FI
STARRY FRONTIER...

". . . Why, you pipsqueak commander of a one-ship armada, Earth does and must control the solar system. She—"

Stan leaned forward and his voice overrode the commander's, his eyes fiercely boring into the—yes, frightened eyes, he realized—before him.

"You don't control any animal but a tame one, mister," he said, and his voice held the grimness of space. "And take this as a dictum: the men of the Asteroid Belt are not tame—not to you, not to anybody. Tame men don't tame space.

"The Belt will never again accept the domination of Earth. And we have the means to back our stand."

Phase Two

Phase Two

WALT AND LEIGH RICHMOND

SF
ace books

A Division of Charter Communications Inc.
A GROSSET & DUNLAP COMPANY
360 Park Avenue South
New York, New York 10010

PHASE TWO

An ACE Book

Cover art by Walter Velez

First Ace printing: December 1979

2 4 6 8 0 9 7 5 3 1
Manufactured in the United States of America

For Scott and Chuck-

"... It takes people who have had to fight and win against their own hostile environment to fight and win against the subversive odds of an overprotective society...."

Aboard the C-Lab
P.O. Box 2016
Melbourne, Florida   32901

Until we had instruments to measure them, we did not recognize that the electromagnetic fields of the planets exist. Because we do not have instruments to measure it, we are refusing to recognize the field of the human body. Yet both are physical facts; the yin and yang of the universal structural pattern.

The human field is a complex configuration of fields; as the body is a complex configuration of atoms. Why, the very atoms of which the body is formed are held in their intricate matrices by the interactions of their individual fields!

———Notes from an Anthropologist

PROLOGUE

New findings in human information input, analysis, storage, retrieval, and use show a complex structure: Input is electronic, analysis is an interface action between the brain and the field computers; storage is biochemical and holographic; retrieval and use are eidetic.

Findings in Centric Analysis
#11764/77

There is no mistaking a Belter when he walks on Earth, though he wears the privacy cloak of planetary custom. The way he holds his head, his stride, the looseness of his carriage, the purpose that seems to spring from his whole being.

The one was tall, his body instinct of an energy of purpose. The other, smaller, round, still with the carriage, still with the stride. The taller wore a con-

1

servative grey cloak that matched well with the crowds in the corridor; the other a golden cloak, flamboyant against the crowds.

Heads turned as they passed.

There were few words between the two as, ignoring the slideways, they strode along the corridors of the top floor of the city complex, toward an office where they were expected.

When the smaller one spoke finally, it was after a glance around; after assuring himself that it was crowded enough that a computer-filter would not pick up key words and record their conversation marked for replay.

"You realize that we will be outmaneuvered; that whatever measures we take, they will retain control?"

"I realize. I do not like it."

"It is necessary. The Belt has not yet developed the know-how in the research sciences to make a pool. The great reservoir of knowledge of the exact sciences is still on Earth. The source of our molecular-information tap is here."

"I know. I do not have to like the facts I know to be true."

"Copies of the molecular-knowledge banks that we create here will get to the Belt. That will be my job."

"Your role as Mentor here is the one part of the contract we must not let them control. Yet, once they have the system, how shall we force them to keep you? A contract with the Belt means nothing to them. And the time of their learning the system may be short. That is the crux. That is the gamble."

The smaller man smiled gently. "We lose nothing. The system will defeat their purpose, no matter whether they use or abuse it. But . . . you must be prepared to accept compromises you know to be disguised defeat."

The other nodded without speaking, and a silence fell between them.

The tension in the big man showed only in the gesture with which he pushed through the door they had finally reached.

The three awaiting them were in privacy cloaks, but each cloak was designed to show the status of its wearer. A professor, a corporate executive, a military man. And each wore in his manner the characteristics of his profession.

It was the corporate representative who greeted the visitors. "Trevor Dustin?" he asked in a high, genial voice. "Known as Trail Duster on the 3-D, I believe," he added with a small laugh.

The tall newcomer nodded, unsmiling.

"And Dr. Katsu Lang," continued the corporate official. "The scientist who developed the molecular memory transfer system."

The smaller, round Belter shook his head. "No," he said. "I am a Mentor. I bring you the development of others, with the hope that we can utilize the training in an Earth school."

The corporate official nodded. "My mistake," he said. "I have trouble following the credit lines of the new sciences, though I seldom have trouble finding a use for their results." He turned to his companions. "May I introduce . . ."

It very quickly became apparent that it was the military man who had the say in the discussion.

Steepling his fingers on the table, the general, introduced vaguely as representing the military forces, made clear his interests.

"If, as you say, you can introduce the knowledge and training of many specialists into the minds of young men by inoculation, without wasting many of the years of their youth, we will indeed back your school to the hilt."

Then he leaned back, and his voice took a commanding note. "However, since our budgets will be sufficient to carry the experimental school—as well as any succeeding schools—I see no value whatsoever in our incorporating"—he paused and looked at the bigger Belter with narrowed eyes—"in incorporating hard-earned Belter credits in the school's establishment."

Trevor Dustin smiled briefly and coldly. "Unless we have a controlling interest, we refuse to release the methods involved." There was no question in his voice.

"That is as it may be," said the general. "Unless we have controlling interest, there will be no such school, either here or in the Belt." Then he leaned forward. "You have a reputation for stubbornness against Earth's legitimate control systems, Dustin," he said. "But the facts of the situation of the Belters in respect to Earth exist; and pressures can be applied."

The two locked eyes. The atmosphere suddenly became electric.

It was the soft voice of the Mentor that broke the impasse.

"It would not go well on 3-D," he said quietly, "were it announced that Earch refused Belter credits, when the military budget is so great a burden on the citizen. I have heard it said, 'A Belter hand doesn't dirty a credit—only a tablecloth.' Our credits must establish our rights in the new technology. It will have advantages in the Belt as well as on Earth."

The military man relaxed back against his chair. "Sounds a bit like blackmail," he grumbled. "You Belters. Stoop to anything . . ."

The Mentor's hand on his arm stilled the first movement of the taller Belter's muscles.

It was the professor who spoke now. "We will need to understand and prove the theories before we question control of those theories," he said. "If the Belters find advantages in the new systems, well and good. If we find advantages, if the theories prove out, we can go from there."

When the two finally left the luxurious office, neither spoke until they had traversed most of the city, using the slideways this time, making their way from level to level.

Finally, in an even voice that betrayed no hint of his anger, Trevor Dustin said, "You will be thrown out as soon as they are convinced the theories are valid; as soon as they have the techniques. And it will not take them long. There was no slightest intent there to let you remain in charge."

The Mentor nodded. "But we have what we must have. Access, if only for a while, to the source. To the reservoir."

"If they find out, they will sabotage the molecular shipments."

Dr. Katsu Lang smiled quietly. "*If* they find out. Copies of the great molecules will get to you so long as I am able to get them to you. Which may not be long. The tensions are great and the variables many."

"They will use the new students as weapons against us!" Trevor's voice was low, but the urgency in his voice might alert a computer recording if it continued. The Mentor rested his hand again, momentarily, on the other's arm, before replying quietly.

"Of course. And so will not achieve the weapon of which they dream. It will be their downfall, one way or the other. If they create robots, as they will, their weapon is meaningless. If they create thinking men, they themselves are destroyed. But, yes, they have the control, no matter what the contracts they have signed, which offer little enough compromise in themselves. Will you go now to see your son?" he asked, changing the subject.

"No. Star must not even know I've been Earthside. The pressures on him already are so great, he may have warped. His mother died."

"You will know soon. I shall start that machinery into motion now."

"And I, in the hope he has survived the youth he was subjected to, shall make a few arrangements, too."

The two saluted one another formally and parted company.

1

*The potential for transferring information direct from one
human to another through RNA innoculation was uncovered
in the 1960s. When information is introduced in this manner, it has bypassed both analysis and field storage and becomes a stimulus/response reaction logic in the body, out fron
under conscious (interface) control, and without the relationality of field logic.*

*——Findings in Centric Analysis
#11864/77*

His name was Stanley Thomas Arthur Reginald
Dustin, and he knew that the acronym was intentional—that it had been "bought" for him by his
uncle at a price.

The name had been registered, the price accepted; but when his mother died and his uncle re-

turned to the Belt, his father's disapproval had registered as well, and he could be known only by his first name, Stan.

"Ruffians make up the bulk of the planeteers," his father assured him as soon as he was old enough to ask. "Ruffians and ne'er-do-wells who can't make it on Earth and have to flee. There is the occasional adventurer like my brother," he added carefully, "but that is the exception. Even so, your Uncle Trevor has behaved beneath the dignity of the family."

The red hair, the set chin, and the gangling length that he had inherited from his uncle could not so easily be disavowed, but that heritage was offset by a pug nose and freckles that were concomitant of nothing more than youth; and with that his father had to be content.

There had been friction between the stern, unbending father and the easygoing, carelessly alive boy from the beginning; an undercurrent of friction that seldom surfaced, that Stan was hard put to understand. But it was his father's determination that one adventurer in the family was more than sufficient, that Stan should be schooled to the responsible position in his own community that his father had created for him; that was the real point of friction between them. That had nearly obviated the possibility of Stan's entering the school on the Arctic slopes where he now sat in a learning cubicle answering test questions on the computer screen before him.

Interminable questions. They made up almost the entire curriculum of the school. Questons, with nothing on which to base his answers. Questions that leapt from subject to subject; that sometimes

centered whole concepts and assumed not only
knowledge from top to bottom of the field involved,
but, Stan decided, intuition within it.

*Given the lens configuration in the diagram above, specify
the index of refraction required in lens C.*

Stan glared at the sentence as though it were an
enemy, but it refused to go away. Yet, as though his
body had a will of its own, he began estimating angles by eye and tapping figures into the hand-held
calculator that was his only permitted tool of com-
putation, while he shifted decimals in his head.

At the same time a wry part of his mind was composing its own completely irrelevant answer: *A lens
configuration in my imagination, might show two chaps
completely out of whack. . .*

"One point three one," he tapped out on the
board, and the lines began to move upward again
*. . . and select from the following list the type and weight
percentage of materials required to formulate such a lens for
operation in an environmental temperature range of 220° to
260° Kelvin.*

Underneath the surface attention he was putting
on the CRT screen, that portion of his mind that
refused to be disciplined went on: *. . . Uncle Trevor
large and bratty; versus Father, trim and natty, and forever
biting Trevor in the back.*

The list of materials on the screen included silica,
soda . . . on through the range of possible combina-
tions for various types of glass, and Stan was reviewing everything he knew, which seemed even to him
to be considerable, about the art of glassmaking.

*With a big computer and about six months' time, perhaps
I might be able to come up with some sort of answer as to the
approximate grade of glass required*, he decided. But
even as he thought it, three-quarters of the way

down the list his eye rested on the simple chemical
formula; H_2O. He glanced back at the top part of the
question: Temperature range, 220° to 260° Kelvin.
Two-twenty Kelvin would be about minus fifty-
three Centigrade, would be . . .

Right. Ice.

The things they expect you to know on a test like this, he
thought ruefully.

This school had been a compromise on both his
father's part and his own. Stan wanted, perhaps because it was denied him, abjectly and unreasoning-
ly but absolutely, the training necessary to ship on
the interplanetary lines. At least that was his stated
ambition—to go out in the ships that plied the system.

What he really wanted, the secret desire that
gnawed his vitals with a desperate yearning, was to
explore the stars. But he knew that to be hopeless—
not because of parental opposition, but because the
laws of nature made it hopeless. Before that became
possible, the Einstein formulas would have to be re-
written—and they'd been proven long ago and over
and over.

That desire was useless and, he told himself severely, it was a sign of immaturity to continue to
harbor it. The fact that his father did not even suspect its existence was hardly surprising. Stan hid it
from himself whenever possible.

His father was not only adamantly against anything that smacked of space, but actually anything
that smacked of technical training.

"As you grow older, you will begin to understand
the value of the money-making systems," he told his
son firmly. "It is all very well to be able to build or
run gadgets; but gadgeteers are a half-credit the

gross. The comfort in which you live is derived and will be derived in any society, from the ability to see that the gadgets are distributed and security assured to the people."

And, thought Stan, even my name was bought—by a bequest from Uncle Trevor that established my father in the comfortable insurance business that keeps us if not among the wealthy, at least among the much better off.

"You shall indeed go to the planets, explore the entire system," Stan's father had explained carefully, "but as a tourist, free to explore; free to sample the best of everything that is offered; free of the slave labor that marks the life of a"—the word was distasteful in his mouth—"a planeteer, or an Asteroid Belter."

The school here was a compromise; his acceptance into its five-year course a surprise to them each. And Stan was not even sure how that compromise had been reached.

The Mentor who had had him called for conference during a late afternoon of his final high school year had been a stranger, and strangely dressed even by the most flamboyant standards.

Stan had entered the conference room cloaked in the normal long grey cloak of privacy over his almost-colorful dark blue singlet and matching hose. He was received by an older man—how old? It was hard to say—in a silken gold tunic belted over trousers of the same soft golden material; and soft gold kid slippers. It was the belt that kept Stan's attention: a gold belt, interwoven in an intricate symbol of intertwined snakes.

When Stan's eyes had finally rested on the man's face, he had found it uncreased, smooth, almost featureless. Eskimo? he'd asked himself.

As though the man had read the question in his eyes, he'd answered softly, "Ainu. An old race with an old tradition. I am Katsu Lang. Won't you throw off the cloak? I expect we will be friends, and no privacy between us."

Startled, Stan had removed the cloak and folded it carefully over a chair.

He had been accepted, Dr. Lang told Stan slowly, in a newly organized school set up under rather special conditions, teaching a "newly developed engineering course." Designed, the Ainu had said, to best equip a candidate for a general understanding of the society and possible usefulness in its further technological development.

"Accepted?" Stan had asked, and been assured that the criteria were rigorous; that he had been found acceptable under the most exacting standards.

He wasn't at all sure how it was that he had quite suddenly become convinced that this five-year course was what he wanted; but he had been quite sure that it was something his father would refuse.

"If you will permit us," the Mentor had assured him, his strange, nearly poreless face without expression, "I believe that this part can be handled for you. If you accept this assignment . . ."

Stan had accepted, and though he was not sure after he'd arrived at the school itself that it was what he wanted—he was here; he had been here over four years; and the challenge was still intense.

Given the necessity to move an object with the mass of one hundred kilograms from an Earth orbital position of five hours forty minutes, to a Martian orbital position of twenty-four hours thirty minutes, select the energy most nearly suit-

able, making the following assumptions . . .

That, Stan recognized, was the classical three-body problem that had bugged mathematicians back about the time that people were first getting into space. But, a deep part of his mind was telling him, the answer is easy when you recognize that the sun is the major reference body. Any object in Earth solar orbit will have a definite energy relationship to the sun, and in order to move it to Mars orbit, it will have another definite energy relationship. Of course, a body around Earth in orbit will also have an energy relationship that must be canceled in relation to that body if you are to leave; and similarly, a body taking up orbit around Mars will achieve a definite energy relationship with Mars. So the whole thing works out as three inter-related problems—not the classical three-body problem. That became an impossibility only when one failed to consider all of the factors involved and tried instead to consider a limited subset of factors.

While his "deep mind" was considering the problem, the imp on the surface was interpolating: *To move an object from A to B, you go to school by the Arctic Sea . . .*

The school! But it wasn't a school, Stan told himself. It was a series of tests. It was nothing but tests, actually, with occasional lectures that seemed more designed to puzzle than inform. The first day's schedule had consisted of nothing but tests, in this same cubicle, on subjects that ranged from engineering to sociology to anthropology . . . any and every subject you could think of. At the end of the tests he had learned that the next day would consist of a similar series, and that he could study for it or not as he liked.

But study what? There had been several areas in the first tests that had left him blank and curious. He started on those in the tiny library cubicle assigned to him; and he'd found that each tape he'd worked through had led him on to other tapes; and pure curiosity had kept him going, on and on. . . .

He'd fallen asleep in his small room, expecting to be called for the next day's assignments, and had not wakened for nearly fourteen hours.

Without even pausing to find out what meals he'd missed, he'd gone straight to the classroom cubicle, where the impersonal quiz program had simply begun on his arrival and continued until he left.

Famished, puzzled, uncertain, he'd left the cubicle and searched until he'd found an office. His knock was answered, and he'd entered to again face the Mentor in the golden suit with the gold belt.

"I . . . overslept."

"Filing time is important, too," the Mentor had said softly.

"I—I haven't eaten. Dr. Lang. I don't know the schedule, I don't know what to study. I haven't met my classmates. I . . ." His voice had run down.

"You will find your classmates in the common room, whenever you care to go there. Your studying seems to have followed a very well selected pattern. The meal schedule is posted in the common room."

"But . . . lectures? Classes?"

"They are posted."

"On what terms will I be kept or dropped? I assume that you don't keep all the students. You said that the course was competitive."

"It *is* competitive. We expect to drop at least three-quarters of the students to lesser courses within the five years."

"You . . . I guess you're sort of leaving it up to each of us how we study and what we do?"

"Isn't that advisable? In selecting for the best, that is? Those dropped will have fine courses and careers ahead of them."

There is no use asking questions, Stan realized. *He's not even going to give me very good hints.* He took a deep breath.

"Your questions—your tests—cover subjects with which I am completely unfamiliar. How do you expect me to answer the questions? How can you expect us to pass the tests?"

"Have you found it impossible to answer the questions?"

Stan found himself blank for a minute. Then, with an effort, he forced himself to recall one of the tests he'd had the day before. A mathematical quiz, and he watched himself sitting before the board, the questions arising one from another, across the screen, as he'd answered them. There were long pauses before each answer; pauses in which he'd strained every mental muscle he possessed to . . . remember? . . . to grasp? . . . to analyze? . . . and the answers had come; feebly and unsurely, but they had come. Correct or incorrect, there had been answers there when he'd reached deep and strained to . . . remember.

He felt exhausted, as though he'd been running for miles and was wilting . . . wilting before the second wind came? he asked himself, standing there before the smooth-faced Mentor, trying to frame the question that would give him the answer to the school itself.

"If a test selection asks something that you do not know," the Mentor said softly, "you can always answer that you do not know. That would be quite a valid answer, would it not?"

I've come this far, Stan told himself grimly. *I shan't be licked by the prospect of endless examinations. And—I shan't be one of those relegated to merely "fine courses and careers."*

"You have had your inoculations?" Again the soft voice carried no inflection other than the queston.

Stan was startled. Inoculations had been part of the entrance proceedings. He nodded, mutely.

"You will have them weekly," he was told. "They will . . . help."

. . . 1. Assuming that time is not important, the question on the board before him continued, and the imp in Stan's mind went back to its interrupted doggerel: *Where you study all questions from Υ to $\mathcal{Z}$, before moving the object from A to B.*

Let's see. If time's unimportant, you use the basic energy level from Earth orbit to Mars orbit, plus the energy level of the Earth orbit to infinity, minus . . . The little calculator gave him figures, and he poked the figures into the keys of the CRT.

The answers were there. Almost invariably, if he reached hard enough. The answers seemed to grow out of the pyramidal structure of the questions— and yet they didn't. He was calling on information he had not known he possessed, and it puzzled him. Yet the catholicity with which he pursued information during the free hours of the day must be the source, he told himself.

The hours between exams—and outside the sleep that seemed to claim him willy-nilly and occupy far more hours than he liked to waste this way—were in the nature of a race. What the next day's tests would cover he never had any idea. So he sought information at first like a Snark seeking Boojum, and, he told himself severely, this won't do. He'd soon found that if one day's tests were on a specific subject, the next day's tests were apt to be on entirely different subjects, so that the tests themselves gave him very little lead.

That fact had thrown him for a loss for a while; and he'd found himself continuing to grab for information in those off-hours in so helter-skelter a manner that he was attempting everything and acquiring nothing.

Five years is a long time, he finally decided. *If a subject is dropped today, it will be resumed in the foreseeable future.* And he began following the subject of each day's tests in that day's studying. It seemed to pay off.

It was the sleep that he continued to fight and that, in its way, continued to fight him. After that first night, it hadn't been a normal sleep—not for a long time. It had been a feeling of sleep that built an increasing tension within until it would seem as though he were bursting; and as it seemed inevitable, in his dreams, that he would burst, he'd wake, to fall asleep again almost instantly and go through the increasing tension again. Hour after hour—and he'd wake exhausted.

It felt as though he were fighting an internal war. He found himself increasing his study hours to avoid sleep; found himself fighting to keep his attention on the library tapes to the point of exhaustion. But exhausted as he might be, at the moment he fell asleep, the tension would begin to build . . . and build . . . until one night he didn't wake and there was what he remembered later as an internal explosion that had continued for some time as a series of minor explosions. They wafted him forward and back, forward and back, as on a constantly reversing current, until he drifted peacefully with it, no longer fighting, no longer tense.

Waking, he felt refreshed for the first time since coming to the school. That night he'd returned to his sleeping room expectant, had fallen asleep to the old tensions, but almost immediately an explosion had occurred—a lesser explosion this time. Then came the forward and backward motion that was as restful as a rocking chair.

The process had gone on for a week, until finally the tensions and the explosions had dropped out, and the rocking motion had begun the instant he'd fall asleep. *My alternating-current sleep,* he'd called it. He looked forward to it now; to the refreshment, greater than any he'd ever known; to the soft currents themselves; to the satisfied feeling with which he'd wake.

His life had taken on a similar alternating-current rhythm. The tests were a flow in one direction as he discovered that if he relaxed and let what he thought of as his subconscious work, the answers came easily; whereas if he strained, they seemed to be stopped.

Studying was the alternate flow, a pursuit of knowledge that was instinct of a furious demand he found within himself for knowledges that came, not from his subconscious, but from his conscious and pursuing mind. The demand was so intense that it seemed to be driven by an internal competition between the two forms of mental activity; to be a crucial race, in which the prize was the survival of the mind; a competitive urge that claimed him daily as he left the testing cubicle and took him direct to the library and its concentrations.

The race left him little time for the common

room, though there were games and conversation to
be had there. On the occasions when he did appear,
it seemed to be full of students, uncloaked and in-
formal, in variations of the dark singlets and hose
that were stylish. He rather assumed that the other
students were taking the same hours he did for studying, and didn't worry about it. What they did
was their business, he decided.

But the lack of privacy cloaks made him uncom-
fortable so long as he thought of the room as a public gathering place. Then, since his own cloak
served no purpose other than to make him conspicuous, he dropped it, rationalizing the move with
a decision that a student body is, after all, like one's
own family. Since he seldom met anyone in the
halls, he took to going to and from the test cubicle
uncloaked as well.

Mostly, though, when he alloted himself time off
—and no one in authority seemed even slightly interested in setting hours or schedules except for the
occasional lectures, meals, and weekly inoculations
—he went topside. He'd discovered the entrance to
the outside once when he went determinedly explor-
ing the school plant, originally an oil refinery complex abandoned when the age of oil ended. There'd
been heavy outside wear—quilted boots and
trousers; hooded and gloved tunics—in the small
room beyond the door that was marked simply *outside*; and he'd helped himself and gone out into the
arctic wastes.

That first time he'd not intended to go far, but
the empty spaces beyond the small entrance held an
enchantment. The sun was on the horizon, bright
and small and making a path across the white expanse that gleamed golden. He followed the path

almost blindly, drinking in the lonely sweeps of snow; a loneliness that he'd never found before; that created a hunger in his entrails. The cold air bit into his lungs, and he fastened his hood to cover his mouth and nose and went on.

Abruptly the sun was gone, and a wind rose violently to sweep snow into his eyes. He kept on for a bit, but the wind gusted harder, and he turned to find the white expanse on all sides; his tracks covered, and no sign of the entrance through which he'd come. A near-panic gripped him, and he stood stock-still for a minute, feeling it wash over him; feeling his body react to panic, the urge to run pull at his legs.

Then he laughed. This, he thought, must be what it was like to be in space. And he looked at the whiteness reflecting back the remaining light and stretching to infinity in every direction, and felt an urge to throw out his arms and embrace it.

Turning in a complete circle, he tried to determine the direction from which he'd come. It was then that he saw the small figure approaching and recognized it instantly by the golden padded suit, shaped like his own, but glowing in the reflected light.

Bracing himself against the gusting wind, Stan went to meet the figure. "Dr. Lang," he shouted through the wind when they were near, "have I done wrong to come out?"

The face that he knew to be broad and expressionless was hidden behind the hood, but as the wind lulled between gusts, the voice was unmistakable. "I think, Stan, that we shall give you a special inoculation. No, you have not done wrong. Should it be wrong to come out into the open?"

A queston for every question, Stan thought. But, "No, it should not be wrong. This is . . ." His words were whipped from him as the wind gusted again, but he went on, knowing that he was not heard. "This is peace. It should be sought."

After that, he'd gone out for at least a little while almost daily. He'd never gotten lost again, and he'd never met the Mentor again. But the trips topside had come to mean a relaxation and a cleansing, more effective than a shower.

". . . 2. Assume that the movement of the object must be accomplished using a standard Class Four Rover in less than eighteen months . . ."

Stan tapped the keys of the hand-held calculator while his mind slipped off in its own channels.

Once he'd gotten hung up on a question so long that a tall, bearded man, properly cloaked, had come along to drag him from the cubicle. It had been one of the few times there'd been any form of —well, interference, and he'd come out in a fury.

"I'm Professor Mallard," the man had told him. "Why the devil have you held so long on this one question? Why didn't you just mark it 'don't know' and go on to the next? Why did you make me come to drag you out?"

"I kept thinking I had the answer," Stan replied, his fury fading as he brought himself back from his concentration to find the school around him. "It was just . . . almost there. And if I could bring enough . . ."

"That question," Professor Mallard had interrupted him acidly, "is a misprint and leads to an open-ended and unsolvable equation. Your insistence on perfection would have done you no slightest good. In the future, have the grace to use the 'don't know' button just a bit less stubbornly."

"*. . . 3. Assuming the use of any known vehicle. The motion must be carried out in less than two weeks.*"

Stan had missed his home and friends at first as the strange course went on; but more and more the trips home had come to seem like visits to a foreign land, the people to speak an alien tongue.

And then, in one short week, his home became enemy territory.

He had barely arrived for Christmas vacation when the news broke on 3-D: ships of the Belt had attacked Earth Fleet; had attacked and destroyed a few of the mighty vessels that controlled interplanetary space.

And the Belt forces were led by Trevor Dustin.

The shock was felt everywhere. It was impossible. The tiny, weak population of the Belt taking on the might of Earth?

But as the hours passed and the 3-D marshaled its on-the-spot coverage from space itself, the shock became greater.

The screens showed the huge battleships of Earth, light-colored to reflect back the impinging rays of the sun; long cylinders more than two hundred feet across, spinning slowly to give gravity when not under thrust. Mighty ships. Their hulls held six feet of water for radiation shielding over the entire surfaces; water that served as a major part of the life-support systems for the crews and the two thousand Space Marines that were the normal complement. They were armed with powerful lasers for space warfare; and with projectile and atomic cannon for planetary warfare, though the ships themselves would never come nearer to a planet than a two-hour orbit. Massive monsters, capable of maneuvering at up to a two-G thrust . . .

And darting among and between them like a flight of stubby crossbow arrows, black so that they were nearly invisible, the tiny ships of the Belt.

"The Belters have dropped their freight doughnuts, and they're using the central control-cabin/thrust-tube segments of their freighters as fighting ships," an excited commentator explained. "They've painted them black so they can't be seen by eye . . . a useless gesture. They can be seen by ladar."

Breathless, he went on, explaining to an Earth audience that had never considered the problems of Belt shipping. "The Belters load their freight into doughnut-shaped containers, the way freight used to be loaded on Earth into the trailer end of a tractor-trailer truck. Their control cabins are directly attached to the ion drive tube that centers any space-ship, and that control cabin is the only part of the ship that needs shielding, since the freight travels in vacuum. When the freightnut is loaded, the control-cabin/drive-tube combination is fitted into its center, and the Belter accelerates it into a Hohmann orbit toward its destination, then lets go. The freightnut is picked up at the far end of its trip by a similar ship/drive-tube.

"Those drive-tube ships are *fast*," he went on. "With no shielding needed except for the small living section, they're long and fast and maneuverable. They can get thrusts up to any Gs a man can take; and the system of dropping the freightnuts makes almost every ship in the Belt a fighting ship."

Then the head of Earth's Space Commission was brought on to reassure the vast listening audience.

"The Belters are getting too big for their britches," he said solemnly. "Of course, they haven't any firepower at all, comparatively speaking; and this uprising should be over in a few hours. They have been listening to the traitorous leaders who have quarreled with Earth's very light and reasonable control measures from the beginning. When this is over, the traitors must be weeded out and restrictive measures taken.

"It may hurt a parent to spank a child," he went on kindly. "Especially an insanely brave child. However, it must be done for his own good. The very act of attacking where there is no possibility of winning shows the extent of the delusions of grandeur from which the Belters must be rescued."

Yet time went on, and the predicted spanking became more and more remote.

The tiny ships of the Belt were everywhere; black mosquitoes diving onto light-colored elephants, flicking their tail-jets at the elephants and pulling out again. They didn't even try to match firepower with their prey; just dove almost onto the Earth ships, then pulled into steep, G-punishing climbs that flicked their tails toward the hulls of their enemy and sprayed them with the full jetstreams of their drives.

A few were swatted, but very few compared to the numbers that were diving again and again. The mighty laser guns of Earth Fleet had been built to focus sharply at distances of two hundred kilometers and better, and were having trouble with their accuracy in this infighting. The Earth gunnery officers did hit their targets, as was demonstrated with fair frequency by minute sparks of light on the target hulls. But the targeting sparks seemed to be without effect except when a spark hit the control-cabin end; and even then it was usually followed by only a tiny puff of steam that was gone almost as soon as it appeared, while the Belt ship arrowed on instead of exploding.

Not so with the stings of the myriad Belt mosquitoes. As the tail of the Belter lighted the hull of its prey with the ghastly blue glow of its jetstream, a great gout of steam would pour forth and continue to spout. It did not take many hullings before the giants dissolved from hydrostatic shock in great soundless blasts of steam and debris on the viewscreens of Earth.

They were strange battles to watch, as the two fleets came together time after time: the ponderous ships of Earth maneuvering majestically, while the tiny Belt ships dove in and out among them, dancing like fireflies at punishing accelerations and decelerations; in patterns impossible for the heavily manned, heavily armored leviathans of Earth.

"Guerrilla ships," the Belters were called by the astounded commentators. Guerrilla ships that were showing a technological invincibility that had not been suspected. Guerrilla ships that were recklessly, impossibly, remaining on the attack—and winning.

It was over in three days; three days in which neither Stan nor anyone else left the 3-D; in which food was something to be gulped between battles; in which sleep was out of the question.

Stan watched the last and crucial fight. The Earth fleet had been maneuvered into massing; and the guerrilla ships were diving through the mass, one after the other, picking off the central ships

while the firepower of the Earth ships was limited
for fear of hitting their own. It was a daring thing to
watch as the one-man Belt ships threw themselves
unhesitatingly into and through the mass of
monsters.

Stan was watching, too, when the flagship of the
Belt fleet, "Traitor Dustin's ship," the commentators called it, as tiny as the others, took a hit and
spun out, away and impossibly away, exploding
slowly in the fantastic silence of a space war. But
with that ship went the Earth Fleet giant, the main
battleship, *Earuna*.

It was over. Earth Fleet had withdrawn to "re-
group and study the situation," the commentators
said, though the euphemism was obvious to even
the most chauvinistic. Earth was defeated, and the
Belt independent.

And Uncle Trevor dead, Stan added to himself,
while the commentators talked excitedly of the unexpected technological abilities of the Belt, which
were matched (they emphasized) by the technology
of Earth, though that technology had not been
thought necessary to the control of the
spaceways. . . .

Stan left the 3-D, but instead of going to his den
to sleep, he took the elevator to the top of the sky-
rise; to the park area, where he could look into the
sky and beyond it.

As he left the elevator, a familiar figure, tall and
heavy under its flapping cloak, was approaching it.

"Hi, Tom," Stan said, preoccupied.

"Traitor Dustin!" was Tom's only greeting, and
Stan found himself ducking a roundhouse right
cross that barely missed his nose, the broad sweep
of Tom's cloak sleeve slapping across his face.

What happened next was as much a surprise to Stan as it was to Tom. He had been attacked. The attack had missed only because of his own quick reflexes which, almost of their own accord, now had Tom engaged in a half-nelson, Stan's left arm gripping a pressure point at the back of Tom's neck.

"What shall I break first?" he heard himself asking in a mild voice.

The overstimulation that should have resulted from a flood of adrenaline to the circulatory system in the standard fight-or-flight response wasn't there. There was none of the raggedness of heavy breathing that would formerly have accompanied any fight. The autonomic responses hadn't been needed or triggered. He hadn't even had his attention on the fight. He was still debating his own fierce pride that the Belt had won. He should be loyal to Earth—or should he? Somehow there was a feeling of justification, both in the war and in his own personal battle that he neither understood nor wanted to question.

The next day he had gone to the tailor and had himself fitted for tunics and trousers of a light gray silken material that held a gold tinge. Then he'd selected a tunic belt of gold—plain gold—though he knew that the tailor, his family and friends, would find the clothes, the color, even the fact of the belting, distasteful.

He'd made his visits home as infrequent as possible after that, and now he felt almost a stranger there. The feeling was mutual.

"You look too much like your former uncle for comfort," his father had remarked on his last trip home. "If I were not assured that this school is training you for one of the higher governmental positions, I should suspect . . ."

* * *

Stan punched the last figures into the board before him, and to his surprise saw it clear completely. Then the questions were replaced with a terse summons:

Student S.T.A.R. Dustin. Report to Professor Mallard in Office 201.

Stan jerked out of the daydreams that had more and more accompanied his tests over the years as he had relaxed to let the answers come easily.

It was a physical jerk that brought him aware of the screen and the cubicle, and the summons staring at him seemed meaningless at first; then an intrusion to be feared.

The almost hypnotic rhythm by which he had worked for more than four years lay shattered around him. He felt as though he were stepping over its shards as he left the cubicle.

2

To properly orient unevaluated information in the human system, it is necessary to put the information into review before the conscious (interface) mind, and then to refile in both the biochemical and holographic data storage systems. A method for doing this is to retrieve the information for study during a period when the critical attention of the analytical configuration is available.

——Findings in Centric Analysis #11964/77

Professor Mallard stood, cloaked but unhooded, behind his desk as Stan entered. His piercing eyes seemed to X-ray the student, and his pursed lips seemed to find what he saw unpleasant.

Stan drew himself up. "Student S.T.A.R. Dustin, reporting as ordered, sir."

The professor's face relaxed, and he allowed a small smile to superimpose itself on the disdainful expression.

"Star Dustin," he said in a clipped voice. "Perhaps the name is prophetic, general."

Startled, Stan turned to find a uniformed figure seated casually behind him, beyond the door by which he had entered.

"So this is the young man." The general eyed Stan from his carrot thatch to new grey-gold slippers, then nodded to himself and rose; a big figure in a carefully tailored uniform. "This is your somewhat independent but exotically educated guinea pig, eh? Well, have no fear, professor. We'll tame him. We've tamed the likes of him and better before. After that, we'll see whether he performs to specifications." He nodded briefly to the professor, ignoring Stan, took cap and gloves from the table beside his chair, and left without another word.

As the door closed behind the general, Professor Mallard almost let the precise smile slip—then replaced it carefully. "You have brought yourself to important notice, young man," he said.

Stan felt an internal stillness that held every sense alert, waiting. There was a sure knowledge of danger beneath the stillness, but it was the lesser of two emotions. There was a dislike of the professor so intense as to be nearly overwhelming. *Why the professor?* he asked himself. *Why not the general?* And he found no answer except the fact.

"I haven't flunked, have I, professor?" he heard his voice asking and knew himself to be asking for time to get his balance; to sort out the emotions that threatened to flood his system.

"Flunked?" Mallard considered for a moment,

then shook his head from side to side. "No. Not
that. A bit too . . . self-motivated, perhaps. But as
the general said . . . He decided to leave the sentence hanging.

Silence. The professor stood immobile, his eyes
boring into Stan's.

He expects me to speak first; to look away, Stan
thought. *He's determined to force me. Why?* His chin
lifted and firmed.

At the gesture, the professor's smile deepened.
"Ah, yes," he said with the casual triumph that
comes with winning a personal bet. "A bit too self-
motivated. However . . ." He let the sentence end
before it had begun, slowly dropped himself into the
desk chair, and tented his fingers on its surface.
Each action was deliberate. Then he began to speak
—lightly, as though discussing a subject of no possible import.

"You will be apprenticed as a marine in the
Earth Space Service," he said. His eyes still did not
leave Stan's, and the effect removed any casualness
engendered by his tone. "You will be in that post
for perhaps half a year. When your . . . obvious
eagerness is thoroughly under control, and because
you have shown yourself rather exceptionally
bright, you will be transferred to more and more
responsible positions. By the time that we are ready
to resubdue the Belt, I expect you to be among the
squad leaders of the effort. By then you should have
a squad completely composed of personnel who
have been molecularly trained as you have been,
and should prove—"

"The Belt?" Stan heard his voice ask. "The Belt
is independent, sir."

The professor brought himself up crisply. "The

Belt is *temporarily* independent. It is, you will realize, a condition that Earth cannot tolerate."

"Sir." Stan paused, marshaling his words. "I should prefer another assignment."

"Oh? Another area of independence, eh? Well, that can be ameliorated before your duty even begins. That can . . ." he relaxed abruptly, his face and tone quieted, and he leaned back in his chair. "Young man," he said deliberately, in the voice with which one would comfort an invalid, "most of us would like to choose our own assignments. But aren't you a little young to be attempting to make your own choice now?"

"I am twenty-four, sir. Nearly twenty-five. And I have loyalties. . . ."

"Ah." The professor nodded. "Trevor Dustin's memory. The traitor mythologized into a hero. Trail Duster. And your nickname is *Star* Duster? What a mistake your parents made! I should have realized." Then, fiercely: "You know, of course, that he would have been captured and hanged if he were not dead already? That he has been hanged in effigy?"

Then the voice relaxed. "Well, the first inoculations you get before going to—never mind." He clamped his mouth with a sudden snap, then smiled again. "We can understand your misplaced loyalties, young man. We can also handle them. You have been accorded a high honor, and it is not one that you will be allowed to refuse. It is an honor that has already been accorded you in part, for you were accepted into this school although your I.Q. was at first thought to be too low. And—"

Stan lost the voice as the happy little imp in his mind took up its inane chanting. *Your I.Q. is low;*

your aspect unpleasing. But they'll stuff you in uniform . . .
The doggerel refused to finish, and the fact irked
him irrationally. *Sleasing?* he thought, but it
wouldn't fit, and he dropped it. The professor's
voice was going on . . .

". . . have implemented that honor more thoroughly than any of your classmates. You have sup-
plemented the molecular training with a self-im-
posed study course. It has had its advantages—and
its very obvious disadvantages can be overcome."

"Sir. If I may interrupt. I should like to talk the
matter over with Dr. Lang."

The professor's face showed another of its abrupt
changes. "Professor Lang," he said distastefully,
"is no longer with us. He has not been with us now
for almost three years."

Stan felt himself sinking, as though a support had
been removed from beneath him, and the feeling
startled him. He'd barely known Dr. Lang. But
he'd trusted him. And Dr. Lang was no longer
here? Somehow Stan had thought of him as . . .
well, as standing in the wings; as watching, as waiting. It was an odd thing to have thought, he reminded himself. He'd seen the smooth-faced Mentor perhaps four times, and exchanged very few sen-
tences with him. Yet the feeling of trust, of familiarity, of . . . Dr. Lang had represented to him what he
thought of as the school. And Dr. Lang had not
been there for most of that schooling.

The professor's voice was continuing, and he
brought his attention back to it. "At any rate,
young man, you have very little choice. The results
the school is obtaining must be demonstrated to the
military in no uncertain terms and as immediately
as possible. We have convinced them theoretically

that with molecular training we can put the wisdom of an older man into the resilient body of a young man on a stimulous-response basis. But theory and demonstration are two separate items. Therefore the demonstration must take place. Once they are convinced, we will be able to do this work on a mass-production basis.

"As our top pupil, you have no choice but to be the demonstration agent—and you will not fail us." Over the precisely composed face, a slight smile was allowed to appear. The voice that continued was more kindly now. "We have made an investment in you of well over a megacredit. That is an obligation that you cannot disregard."

Stan was startled. "A *megacredit,* sir?"

"That is correct. Later, mass production will bring the costs to a reasonable figure, but experimental work comes high."

"I . . . " Stan paused. Then: "You keep saying 'molecular training.' May I ask, sir, just what sort of training I have had? I thought—"

"You thought! You were not supposed to think!" The professor's voice was almost a snarl, but immediately he brought it back under control and allowed the slight smile to recompose itself over his severe features, in spite of the annoyance that threatened his composure.

He hadn't wanted this particular youngster, yet the choice had been forced on him. The general was getting restless, demanding a sample of results before any more money would be forthcoming. A demonstration was a necessity.

The other students—any of the other students— would make the specified robotic soldiers. But to *demonstrate* the effect, you needed . . . well, the type

of initiative this—this *Dustin* had shown. You
needed someone who would respond correctly in
the tests, but who had—yes, the initiative to answer
questions on his own; questions specifically about
his training. So he was stuck with the choice. Even
so, it was not a characteristic to be encouraged, so
he went on:

"The training you have had did not *require* thinking; and the insistence you have placed on independent study has gone far toward nullifying the results
we had every right to expect. However, it has also
enhanced certain aspects that are valuable for the
moment. The rest we can alter later. But you must
not forget—you must not be *allowed* to forget—that
it is the molecular training that has given you the
education and the abilities of which you find yourself possessed."

"Am I allowed to know," the boy before him was
choosing his words carefully, "just what this
molecular training is? Of what it has consisted?"

"You will be questioned on the subject, and you
must know enough to answer those questions in-
telligently. Yes." Mallard leaned back in his chair
and his voice took on a lecture-platform quality.

"You have been trained by molecular memory
transplant. The inoculations you were given were of
memory molecules, produced originally by minds
thoroughly schooled in each of the disciplines to
which you have been subjected." He leaned forward again, and again tented his hands on the desk
before him. This explanation was a familiar one. He
had used it effectively on the military, on prospec-
tive donors. It came easily to his tongue.

"These memory molecules are extracted from
trained and dedicated persons in each discipline.

They are then duplicated in the laboratory and returned to the original donor. Any of the duplicates may be substituted with equal success. The donor loses nothing but a few blank days during which the majority of his memory molecules are sorted and duplicated and then reinstalled. And even should the reinstalling, by some misfortune, not be complete, the infinite filing system of the body's biochemical processes can reduplicate and replace throughout the donor's system from the molecules that have not been extracted, and in a matter of weeks."

Stan listened in growing amazement to the statements, recalling the memories of the tests, the search for answers that seemed to be right there but not quite within reach, and their sudden appearance. He had thought he was drawing facts and abilities from his "subconscious," but . . .

"But, sir. I understood that memory was an electronic, not a molecular function. That it was a function of the brain itself. . . ."

"Ah, yes. The electronic brain function as against the biochemical body function of memory storage. The brain function of information selection and patterning, as against the eidetic but stimulus-response memory of the DNA-RNA memory storage system."

The professor was pleased with himself now. Stan might not be the student he would most wish to see succeed, but the work of the years would be demonstrated, and his efforts culminate in the recognition that he—yes, *he* deserved. There was pleasure in his voice as he went on:

"The research is new. As far as we can tell, the old educational system of study, which required information to be filtered through all the senses of the entire human system, gave the student conscious control of the knowledges and abilities he acquired. Whereas our molecular-training implants, introduced directly and only into the biochemical literal-logic circuits of the body's filing systems, produce a stimulus-response basis on which the knowledge is available. An even more thoroughly stimulus-response reaction than a subject of hypnotism exhibits to a posthypnotic command. And," he added, the pleasure in his voice becoming more pronounced, "it is this automatic and predictable reaction for which we are training."

The professor paused, nodding his head slowly. "You can see that the normal response of an older person to any situation calling for his knowledge and abilities would be quite different from that of a young man. No matter how he was cautioned, the young man would respond as a young man, with all the misplaced ideals that lack of experience dictates; with all the impetuous disregard for established patterns that is normal to youth. What we need is youngsters, primed with knowledge and trained abilities, who will use those knowledges and abilities the way an old man would use them: with caution, with due regard for accepted methods of operation, with due respect for his superiors.

"With this molecular-memory-training system, we will be able to fill the action posts of government and the military with young men who will react dependably to almost any situation not only with the most extensive knowledges and abilities that experts have achieved, but in the manner that would be dictated by those same elderly, disciplined minds!"

"In other words, Stan said slowly, "what you are doing here is creating educated robots?"

Mallard found himself jerked back to the realities of the moment. He stared at the boy. "That's a harsh term," he said finally. "But, yes, in its way. What we are doing is putting the education and discipline of mature minds into young bodies. You may find this emotionally upsetting at first," he added kindly, "but consider. You have an education and abilities that could have been given you in no other way. You have a range of knowledge that no one person could have attained in one lifetime; and you have acquired this while you are still young. If the knowledge and abilities are not exactly under your control, why—in the military no one is under his own control, anyway, so what loss?"

Stan found his emotions chaotic, fear predominant; but was not convinced. If he were, in fact, a robot, why must it be for the military?

Then anger surged. Their puppet, was he? But he'd studied—for himself, of himself, by himself, and that was not puppetry. There had to be a way to find out whether, essentially, he was indeed what they supposed him to be. But it would take time.

"I—I'll need some time to think this whole thing over," he said weakly.

"Of course you will, my boy." The professor nodded to himself. "You have had a strenuous course, and will need a bit of relaxation. So you are being given a two weeks' leave to return home and enjoy yourself. Then you will report back here for a short preinduction training, and will be taken to Greateryork for your first assignment. You've not been drawing against your student's credit balance, so you have in excess of two thousand credits to spend any way you wish before you report to your new post. Enjoy yourself. You will be quite busy for a while after you return, so enjoy your leave."

Accepting the professor's smile and nod as a dismissal, Stan left the room. *Pep talk's over and I'm to swallow the fact that Authority has made me a guinea pig without my knowledge,* he thought. *And, I imagine, without my father's knowledge, either. I'm supposed to swallow it with pleasure and feel obligated to go right on being a demonstration guinea pig for the rest of my life.*

The bitterness of the thought surged through him. But, he asked himself honestly, *would you change the situation if you could? Would you forfeit having had the course?* And he knew he wouldn't.

The resentment was there, but the knowledge was there, too. Knowledge in fields that had each taken a man his entire lifetime to acquire. *The knowledge is there,* he told himself. *And I got most of it from Professorburgers.* But he found himself fiercely glad that he'd studied as hard as possible; that there was knowledge there, too, which he had gotten for himself.

There's that, too, to add into their equation, he told himself. *That with which to salve my pride. And what has pride to do with it, anyhow?*

His thinking was still caught between resentment and pride by the time he was aboard the tubecar that would whisk him through the vacuum-tunnel system.

The car, round to fit like a bullet into its vacuumed gun barrel, accelerated at its normal one-quarter G, as each of the magnetic coils with which the tube was wound gave it a pat on the back as it passed. The cars were accelerated by these pats to supersonic speeds in feeder tubes before being shunted into the main lines; were shunted out again through exit tubes and decelerated, each to its dialed destination.

Effectively the tube system was a vast underground induction/repulsion linear motor network serving the transport needs of the heavily populated world in a rapid and unobtrusive manner. Its versatility was such that it served for everything from vast tanker to individual carrier. Its speed made it a more rapid and far safer transport system than train or plane or truck or automobile, and it had replaced them all with a network that extended from the great transpolar trunk lines, through hemispheric tubeways, down to the tiniest of capillary networks that serviced intracity traffic.

Most people "owned" their own tubecars on the same basis that they "owned" their screen phones, parking them in tube-parks beneath each sky-rise or major building, or beneath the few individual homes. In the same manner, corporations "owned" their own fleets of freight or tank tubes. Others depended on public tubecars, available on signal in a myriad of sizes and kinds, for individual, group or freight transport. It was a satisfactory system, patterned after that of the old telephone system, and at least as efficient.

Having inserted his credit card and dialed his destination, Stan would be delivered direct, in this same tubecar, to the tubeport beneath the sky-rise that was his home in Elko, Nevada, more than two thousand miles away, in under two hours.

Home. He'd thought of it through his childhood as open and free, with its sky-rise buildings separated by several acres of trees and playgrounds and fresh air; with the vistas of distant mountains giving

the feeling that there was some real space in the
world, even when you knew the mountains themselves to be thoroughly inhabited.

A nostalgia for the open wastes of snow and ice
topside at the school shook him, and he drew his
cloak of privacy more tightly around him, though
he was alone in a two-seater. He'd always had
privacy. It was the factor given top priority in a
crowded civilization. But space—that was another
factor, and a different thing entirely; and he'd
found himself drinking it in in his daily trips up and
out into the intense cold and intense aloneness
topside at the school.

He wanted to think. He wanted desperately to
think. But his mind refused to function, though the
doggerel that had been its spontaneous accompani-
ment as long as Stan could remember was busy
composing.

*The brain is intelligent; memory's not; it takes what it's
given and functions by rote. If you want to think new
thoughts, bring them in through your head—or be like a
robot and better off dead.*

Suddenly he knew he was not going home. Not
just yet. Five percent of the credits given him as student aid were spent; but the other credits were un-
touched yet, and they'd take him where he wanted
to go, keep him for at least a few days—a few days
in which he could watch the tugs that took off for
space.

He looked at the map of the tube network on the
screen of the car before him, saw by the tiny light
that marked his position that he was already in the
main Alcan/Europe tubeway that carried most of
the traffic across the pole; and nearing Anchorage.

He leaned toward the small keyboard beneath

the map and pushed the button marked CHANGE
OF DESTINATION. Then he inserted his credit
card into the slot beside the keyboard.

With a click the keys of the board loosened so
that they could be used, and he punched out
carefully: *White Sands*. Then, glancing at the map,
he added the coordinates given there.

The action put the invariable record into the
computer for anyone who cared to ask through Information Retrieval. A record that said always, of
everyone, where they went, where they could be
found, what they spent, for what.

But who would care to ask? He was a student,
with two weeks' leave and a fistful of credits to
spend as he pleased.

3

Input information systems are electronic, both through body and field senses. Input information is received at the interface between the body and field computers, where it is analyzed and prepared for ready access or long-term storage in both the biochemical and holographic filing systems. The input system is about one-third faster than either of the filing systems. This necessitates the sleep cycle, during which the filing and storage systems catch up on the information readied for filing.

——Findings in Centric Analysis
#111064/77

Stan arrived at Termdock, White Sands, and made his way to a visitors' gallery from which he could watch the vast tarmac on which the space tugs landed and took off.

For an hour he watched in fascination as the stubby-winged aerodynamic needles, skirted like old women for their ground-effect takeoff, flashed by on their twenty-five mile ground run.

The real activity of the port was invisible from here, restricted to the mile after mile of underground warren that subsurfaced the field itself. In those cavernous warrens would be the mountains of freight being fed up to the waiting tugs through moving belt loaders. There would be the few passengers and the many workers; the rebuilding and repair; the bargaining and sweating, cursing, bribery, cajolery; the vast kaleidoscope of motion and sound that made up the background of trade between Earth and the system.

Above, Stan had seen two takeoffs and three landings while he watched; and it had left him unsatisfied.

Why had he come here, anyhow? he asked himself. To think. To think—and to be near the ships that were reaching out; to be near the fact of space.

But he felt shuttered from it; felt as barriered as . . . as a robot, he told himself.

He straightened away from the rail abruptly. He had plenty of credits to his card, didn't he? And seven hundred of those credits would get him freighter-tug passage, round-trip, to Orbdock. At least there he'd be in space itself, or nearly. At least there he'd see the real freighters, the ships that went into the system, not just their servicing tugs.

* * *

Stan entered the freight tug with his hood up so that the excitement that boiled in him would be disguised, but all the pilot saw was another privacy-mad stupe of a suburban Earthie. He gestured to the acceleration couch beside his own.

"And keep that damned cloak out of my way," he said, not bothering to hide his casual contempt.

The boy's flush was not completely hidden by the hood that shrouded his head, but he only asked timidly, "Don't planeteers wear cloaks?"

The question didn't merit an answer, the pilot decided, and only replied, "Hmmmph," then busied himself over his controls.

Stan restrained an impulse to throw back his hood, to make himself one with the ship and its skipper, contenting himself instead with studying the pilot.

He was perhaps thirty-five, with a mobile face over a wrinkled uniform. His every gesture was alert and intent on what he was doing. The gestures were quick and sure; the hands . . .

Stan's eyes followed the hands to the controls they were manipulating, and a feeling of familiarity tugged at his senses. Alert now himself, he leaned forward. That would be the skirt control; there the dials indicating atmospheric density; that the rate-of-approach indicator; there . . . His hood fell back and his cloak loosened without his noticing the fact.

"Belt in. We're taking off." The pilot didn't even look at his passenger as he strapped himself into the padded chair.

The surge of acceleration was less than that of a tubecar; but it thrilled along Stan's every nerve, and he watched the great tarmac move past, then fly past, and finally flash past as the tug reached mach speeds; felt the surge as the needle-ship went through the sonic barrier as though bursting a brick wall with a karate blow, and flew beyond it, free. He saw the pilot's sure hands flash first to the vanes which angled them suddenly upward, and then to the skirt controls which withdrew those ground-effect wrappings into the belly of the craft.

Earth fell away, and Stan, who had seen it fall away in this manner a hundred times in 3-D dramas, exulted in the difference of the fact from the fantasy; saw, eventually, Earth like a ball to his vision and himself the still center of the blackness of space. They were an ecstasy of factors, those differences. *A robot, am I?* he thought. *I'll get my own experiences!* But it was a small thought, far at the back of his mind, as his senses drank in the facts of flight.

* * *

Orbdock is mile after mile of an interlocked gridwork of air-stiffened tubing, floating in space.

The zero-G plastiplex is centered by a six-hundred-meter plastic doughnut that spins slowly to give gravity to the offices and restaurants and trading halls, the repair shops and maintenance and living facilities that are the nucleus of the dock.

The doughnut itself is the only conventional shape. The gridwork looks like a haphazard concoction of tubes and ships and freight-nets; of catchalls and working areas, strung beyond the central doughnut-like loose spaghetti and buzzed about by tiny workers' scooters.

Freight and passengers arrive from Earth on the ubiquitous tugs which dock at one side of the complex, where they tether to the longest tubes of the grid.

The freight is transferred through the tubes by fan-powered pneumocars, directly to the interplanetary ships that berth on the far side of the complex. These ships, spherical, with ion-drive tubes through their centers, look like huge baloons

with sticks through them; or like some form of alien
insect which hangs, as though disdaining the complex itself, at the very tips of the tubes through
which each is fed its tonnage of food, air, and water,
of freight and people; through which it is nourished
and sustained, delicately sipping until, sated, it
moves slowly off on the lightest of pulsed thrusts,
getting its distance before unleashing the powerful
impetus that will accelerate it to respectable velocities for its journeying.

The passengers are transshipped through the
tubes by pneumocar, too, but usually go first to the
spincenter doughnut. The pneumocars enter at the
axis where the change from nonrotating gridwork to
rotating doughnut can be most easily made; then
dive down one of the spokes, letting off dock personnel at the various levels, carrying the ships' passengers to the more comfortable half-G rim area.

Stan stepped out of the pneumocar into a shrub-
and flower-bordered area that held a restaurant on
one side, an information booth on the other. He
made his way into the restaurant and chose a small
table near the wall, his eye caught by its clear
plastic and the aquarium beyond. He knew the water was for shielding from the strong radiation of the
sun out here beyond the atmosphere; that it also
served as a major part of the air- and waste-recycl-
ing system, and that the fish were part of that system, too. He knew that the water was flowing past
in six-foot-deep rivers, its motion creating the spin
of the doughnut he was in, that gave him gravity.
But the serenity of the fish, of the plants stirring in
the river's motion, belied the fact.

There could be no viewpoints as such within this
shielding, but huge screens showing the complex

beyond gave the illusion of windows; though the scenes were all still, the arrival and departure of tugs or ships almost the only visible activity, and those might or might not occur as he watched.

The floor beyond the open restaurant seemed to slope up from him on either side, though he felt as though he were sitting on the level. And the people were reacting to the very slight coriolis effect by walking a bit more erect than would be normal.

The people seemed to be mostly ships' personnel or dockworkers, in uniforms of various styles and kinds; some neat, others looking used and rumpled. He felt conspicuous. There were cloaks to be seen, but very few, and those obviously tourists. Earth tourists, Stan thought, surprised at the distaste that went with the thought; and realizing with revulsion that the category included himself and that his cloak was the mark that categorized him.

He sat for hour after hour and let his senses simply absorb the scene: the light gravity, the complex, the space beyond and between its network; the smell of recycled air, the movement, the talk around him, the soft music—the feel of an orbital station. He felt drugged with the new sensations, drugged and content to sit, unthinking.

And then, as though a switch had closed, his mind turned on; his emotions, held in leash since he had left the school, would no longer be denied.

Over a megacredit, the school has spent on me, and I am obligated for that, he found himself telling himself. *Or am I? I didn't bargain for the investment, though I'm glad I've got it—extra knowledges, be they robot or my own.*

But shall I be a guinea pig for the rest of my life? Let them manufacture me into a complete robot? A megacredit. Is that what a lifetime is worth?

And while he talked to himself, he felt the tug of the ships he had watched all afternoon. *Man will never reach the stars,* he thought. *That's been shown by the equations. But . . .*

But oh, the free, untrammeled spaces between the planets!

Yet, was the Belt a free man's area? He didn't know; he had no way of knowing. The Belt had won its independence in a daring and individualized fight; his uncle had fought to win that independence and died for it. Yet had the freedom he had won survived the hazards of necessity the Belt itself imposed? Survived the fact that to stay alive a man must be enclosed in atmospheres built and designed for man? And was that so very different from being enclosed in a privacy cloak, the only protection against an environment too crowded to be meant for man?

The 3-D told of slaves in the Belt, working and sweating because there was no "outside," no "topside," to which they could escape. The 3-D told of hardship and privation. But Uncle Trevor— Trail Duster Trevor—he'd been a proud man and a strong one, with a strong laugh . . .

Stan remembered the only time he'd seen his uncle after he was old enough to remember the details. He'd been tall and strong, swinging the youngster into the air and then onto his shoulders, as though physical contact were not something to be avoided. Stan had been scared at the time, but he'd responded after a minute to the hard hands that lifted him; to the feel of flying through the air; to the height of his uncle's shoulders; to the exhilaration of roughness and . . . yes, to the physical contact itself.

You don't make slaves of that sort, he told himself now.

He remembered the taste of fear as his uncle bent down, and the rough hands took him up in the delicious freedom of flying. *Freedom and fear,* he thought now. *Would freedom always carry the connotations of fear?* He supposed it would. Freedom was bought by a man at a price, and only a stupid man refused to recognize the price as he demanded the commodity.

"Get yourself an education, boy," the big man had told him, roughing the red hair so like his own. "But don't let 'em make you a sissy while they're giving you an education. Do your own thinking while you get the information you need, boy. Then come on out to the Belt. I'll have a berth for you; but you're going to have to get yourself there, you know." Then he'd added, half under his breath, "And you not even old enough yet to properly remember."

The small boy had remembered; and the twenty-four-year-old remembered now with a nostalgia that was overwhelming.

Guinea piggery; and for the military at that. . . .

With a rejection that was almost bigger than he could contain, Stan flung himself to his feet.

At the gesture a man at a nearby table looked up.

"Where's the hiring hall? Here or on Earth?" Stan asked him abruptly.

The man, hard-faced, hard-muscled, in rumpled coveralls, looked Stan up and down—the soft student's hands; the quiet student's face; the crisply cut hair; the cloak . . .

"It's up here. Level five, quadrant three," he said disdainfully. "But a fat lot of good it will do the likes of you."

Stan nodded his thanks curtly. "You might be surprised, sir," he said, and was himself surprised at the title he'd given the surly spacer, though he felt justified in giving it.

The hiring hall turned out to be in a much lighter G area, a barn of a room, filled with figures of every description: uniformed and coveralled; neat and slovenly; none cloaked. All had what Stan had come to think of as the spaceman's look; a hard, almost blank expression. An inner absorption, or just blankness?

High on the walls, constantly shifting lights listed the names of ships in dock, their destinations and their needs in the way of personnel. Occasionally a loudspeaker called a name and an office number, and a figure would rise and make its way to one of the cubicles.

"Where do you sign up?" Stan asked the nearest figure, a small man with a wizened face and sharp eyes that surveyed him again disdainfully.

"Application boxes there," the man told him after the survey, nodding toward a series of booths against the wall behind him that closely resembled the test cubicle in which he'd spent so many hours at school.

Inside it was nearly the same—a seat, a desk, a CRT screen; except that the seat was of air-support plastic; the desk a harder plastic; and instead of a keyboard into which you punched your answers there was a glass plate on which you wrote, on which you pressed your fingers for printing; a scanner for retinals.

Name and number. Fingerprints. Retinals. Main area of training. Stan thought a minute, then entered *engineering*. Preferred destination. Without hesitation, Stan wrote *Belt City*. That was all.

There was a pause, then the screen cleared and a metallic voice came to him through a tiny speaker: "Take a seat in the hiring hall. You will be called."

He found a seat near the application booths and waited. From this part of the spincenter there were no viewscreens. He watched the crowd. He slept. He woke and watched the crowd again. He grew hungry, but he ignored the hunger.

He was asleep again when his own name, coming over the loudspeaker, woke him. "S.T.A.R. Dustin," the voice was chanting. "Report to office seventeen."

The office he entered was tiny and bare except for a desk and two plastic puff chairs. Behind the desk sat a heavy man, erect even in the sagging softness of the pneumochair. His face held a hauteur that spoke of authority. He was cloaked, but the hood was back. Stan was relieved. At least his own cloak —he had thought of discarding it but had lacked the courage—wouldn't be held against him.

"I'm Stan Dustin," he introduced himself.

The man looked him over carefully. "I gather you want to work your way to the Belt?"

Stan nodded and remained silent, standing.

"Sit down, sit down." The man gestured to the chair by the desk. "I'd have recognized you even if your identity hadn't been checked quite thoroughly," he said. "You resemble your late uncle Trevor Dustin quite remarkably." Stan started but remained silent. "I gather your decision to go to the Belt is irrevocable? Have you notified your parents?"

"I haven't notified anyone," Stan said, his heart sinking. "I rather thought I'd let my father know after I was gone. I hope it won't be necessary to your hiring—"

"Probably wise from your point of view," the man interrupted. "I assume that any sane family would discourage you."

"I hope that it's not going to discourage you, sir, from—"

The man looked at him quizzically. "It is not my business to be encouraged or discouraged," he said. "I have the quite dubious honor of representing your late uncle. Did you think I was a hiring hand?"

Stan nodded, crestfallen.

The lawyer shook his head in annoyance. "A lack of perception that will not get you far," he said cruelly. "However, that is not my purview. Young man, your uncle left instructions that if you decided, quite on your own, to go to the Belt, and initiated action in that direction, I was to see to it that you got there. So I've taken passage for you on a Mars freighter that raises within the hour. Naturally, relations being what they are, you can't go to the Belt directly; but Mars is a free port. At Mars you will transfer to a Belt freighter. I have the passages here."

Stan found that he was both pleased and disappointed. Why disappointed? he asked himself. Was he trying to prove something?

The lawyer looked at him distastefully, as though he could read the boy's thoughts. "Perhaps you could sign on as a member of a ship's crew. Probably not. But most certainly the technicalities of signing on would alert your family and any others who might be interested in delaying or preventing you.

Which is why," he went on dryly, "I have seen fit to drop everything, charter a space taxi, and get here, preferably before you left Orbdock, for the privilege of seeing you off at the earliest possible moment and before you involved yourself in some mess from which I must extricate you. However I may feel personally, I am professionally charged with getting you to your destination, and I should prefer that the charge did not involve us together in legal technicalities that might link our names for years."

Stan said stiffly, "I did not mean to seem ungrateful, sir. I—"

"But you wanted to run away on your own? Well, it's a fine fat attitude with little that is practical to recommend it. However," he went on before Stan could interrupt, "I am quite sure that I am not doing you a favor in assisting you in getting to the Belt.

"You will have to leave your Earth credit balance as it stands. If you draw it down to zero, or even draw heavily on it while at Orbdock, the computers will automatically be alerted and start an investigation which will delay you. When you get to the Belt you will find that Belters are an intolerant breed, not given to lightly accepting gifts, such as yourself, from Mother Earth. Neither is Earth apt to accept you back lightly, should you fail in the Belt. You will be very much on your own. Do you still wish to go?"

"I'll take my chances," Stan said defiantly.

The lawyer harrumphed. "Well, traitor's blood is traitor's blood, and you are like your uncle in actions as well as appearance."

Stan flushed and started to speak angrily, but the lawyer gestured at him to be silent. "This business is as unpleasant for me as for you. Let us get it over and done with. There is also a bequest here for a thousand shares in a small Belt enterprise which your uncle founded. Whether it still exists, I do not know, but I do not think you should build any hopes on it. Your uncle's death left the corporation in the hands of two partners who may or may not be surviving themselves; and it is an enterprise which may or may not have survived. The shares are yours, for what they may be worth. The corporation is called Astro Technology."

Having finished his business, the lawyer abruptly hooded himself and left the room without a farewell.

Stan stood gazing at the passage vouchers and the shares of stock lying on the small desk. Then he pulled his travelcase from the greatpocket of his cloak and stuffed the papers inside, zippering it carefully.

It was as he started to put the case back into the greatpocket that the realization came.

The Belt, he thought. *I'm going to be a Belter now.*

A grin came over his face; his chin lifted; and with a huge shrug he dropped the cloak from his shoulders, letting it fall to the floor. Stepping over it, he walked out of the office.

4

In the normal process of human living, information received is evaluated before being filed. However, information received during periods of unconsciousness, anesthesia, hypnosis, or heavy emotion—when the interface or conscious mind has been ruptured—has bypassed the analytical process. Unevaluated information retrieved for use from the body or field filing systems is acted on by the human configuration as though it had been analyzed.

Information received by inoculation has bypassed not only the analytical process, but has not been filed into the field system; and is therefore acted on by the body alone in the stimulus/response manner of a robot.

—Findings in Centric Analysis
#111164/77

Stan reached Orbdock, Mars, still preoccupied with his own chaotic emotions and the changing vectors of a lifetime of habitual thinking and reaction.

The change had been accelerated and made easier by the fact of being in space, and by the new sensations and information that his senses were absorbing; but his real attention had been on finding out just what his own basic precepts were, or could be; and the experiences and the information flowed by, almost unnoticed to his preoccupations.

Spincenter at the Mars Orbdock was small compared to Earth's, the doughnut a mere sixty meters in diameter, the gravity at the rim only one-sixth G; but Stan, who'd been in one-tenth G acceleration all the way, was used to it by now and stepped confidently from the pneumocar when they reached the rim.

It was more barren here than on Earth, although the walls were clear plastic and showed the same aquarium beyond. Past the usual restaurant he could see what must be the information center, sloping sharply up from him, a big board on its wall with changing names and numbers on it. He turned in that direction to see a man coming toward him in red skintights with matching red kid slippers, his waist belted in gold worked in the pattern of a snake.

The outfit fascinated Stan, and he found his eyes returning again to the figure as he made his way toward the big board in the distance. To his surprise, the man was approaching him.

"You Dustin?"

He was larger than Stan, blond, and apparently of about the same age. Perhaps a little older. Heavy in the shoulders, slender of waist, and lithe in his movements as he approached. His face looked puzzled.

"Yes, but how did you know?"

"Well, your ship's in, and I've been waiting for you. You're not Mars-clad, but you're not Earth-clad, either. It was a guess. I understood you were from Earth?"

Stan felt minutely proud of his gold-tinged gray tunic and trousers, which were more in the nature of the red-suited man's clothing than either Earth or Mars style.

"I'm Dustin," he reaffirmed. "Stan Dustin."

"I'm Paulsen. Skipper of the *Sassy Lassie*. I reckon you're my passenger for Belt City. I've been waiting for you. Been ready to scat for the past three hours. You ready? That all your duffel?" He nodded at the travelcase Stan was carrying.

"That's all of it," Stan answered.

"If you have a yen to look over Marsport, you'll have to catch the next freighter. The *Marjorie* is due in a couple of days. You want to wait for her and see the sights?"

Stan grinned. There was an air of defiance in Paulsen's attitude. Or perhaps intolerance? Whatever it was, he was obviously prepared to shake Stan at the slightest excuse.

"I'm ready," he said quietly.

"Okay. I'm tied up at Tube 109."

Paulsen turned and strode swiftly to the pneumocar that Stan had just left. Stan entered in time to see him punch out a destination on the controls, and the car started accelerating up through the doughnut, through its spoke to the hub, then angling off on an increasing acceleration toward the tip of the tube where Paulsen's ship would be anchored some ten kilometers away. Deceleration caught him unexpectedly, and he found himself swaying forward in his seat.

The pneumocar stopped, and Stan was floating

in null G. Grasping the seat ahead of him he pulled
himself behind Paulsen to the opening of the car
which was locked onto the *Sassy Lassie's* air lock.

He saw Paulsen pause a second, then push
through the opening, and as the skipper moved
from before him, he could see two other figures in
the air lock, each hand-held into place from one of
the straps on the cylindrical walls. Stan pushed
himself in to join them, carrying his travelcase.

The angled figures of the four in the air lock
seemed eerie and unreal to senses schooled to gravity; but the two grim-faced men were very real indeed.

"This Dustin?" one of the two asked Paulsen.

"Yep."

"You just lost a passenger. He's wanted on
Earth."

Finding a handhold, Stan held himself immobile,
watching Paulsen, who glanced at him briefly,
glanced at his belt, then turned back to the other
two.

"Charges serious?" Paulsen asked.

"How should I know? Some school on Earth sent
orders."

"School? Dustin, what's the problem?"

Stan found himself answering in normal, unhurried tones. "I guess the school I left doesn't like the
idea that I prefer the Belt," he said quietly.

"Still want to go with me?"

"Yes."

Paulsen turned his head again to the other two
and his voice was grim. "You interfering with a
Belter in the normal pursuit of his business?" he
asked.

"Dustin's no Belter."

"He's my passenger."

Stan grinned to himself. Then, releasing his travelcase, which continued to float inconspicuously at
his side, he said pleasantly, "I sure wouldn't want
to cause you unnecessary trouble, skipper. Come
on, boys." And with that he pushed himself back
through the entrance to the pneumocar.

Just inside, he held himself out of the way so that
the two following him could enter the car. Then,
turning his head, he noted the travelcase still floating in the air lock.

"Oh. My duffel," he said happily, and pushed
himself back into the air lock, angling his motion
toward a large red handle marked *Emergency Pressure
Release*.

His fingers grasped the handle before anyone
could react, and he used it as a lever to set his feet
against the side of the lock and pull against his own
leverage.

Abruptly the air spilled from the lock, and with a
thwummp the tube bulkhead closed. Stan, timing the
lowering pressure by a feeling of internal expansion,
had just let go the handle when Paulsen reached
him.

"Get your hands off that dump switch. You'll
have us in vacuum," he said with a snarl.

Stan pushed away to the bulkhead handle, tested
it. It refused to budge.

*"But they're on the other side, and they won't be coming
back,"* he said with a grin, surprising himself since
he'd never spoken doggerel out loud before. *"The
pressure's triple out there, and the door won't budge a
crack."*

Paulsen looked at him in complete disbelief. Then
a smile crept over his face. "Well, there's not
enough pressure in here for comfort very long," he

said, and began cycling them through into the ship proper.

The trip to Mars hadn't prepared Stan for the control cabin of the *Sassy Lassie*. It was clean, but it had a used and battered look. It had been repaired and rerepaired, and it very definitely had the feel of being lived in. There were two decks for living quarters beneath this one, before you got to the ion-drive tube, Stan realized; but it was normally a one-man ship and the skipper probably spent most of his time up here.

The freight doughnut which he knew to be around the ship below was useless to them except in spacesuits. It was vacuum and unshielded; so that this eleven-meter-tall, approximately six-meter-wide extension of the rocket tube was the "ship" as far as people were concerned; and of that space, the hull shielding left only a cylinder seven meters tall with two-and-a-half-meter radius for living quarters.

Stan pulled himself over to the acceleration chair beside the pilot's without waiting to be told, and strapped himself in. Paulsen was already busy releasing the ship from the docking tube so that it would drift off, "Before we get boarders," he said lightly.

"Thanks for the backing, skipper," Stan said carefully in reply.

"You do pick the damnedest times to recite poetry," was Paulsen's answer. "Your air dump used up about one hundred credits of air. Since we don't want to stop for it here, I'm traveling at low pressure, just to be on the safe side of our emergency supplies."

There was silence as Paulsen warmed the motors, nursed small pulsed thrusts to give them distance, and finally cut in power to the drive to give them the normal one-tenth G acceleration. Then he pulled the log toward him and began to write.

Stan let his eyes wander around the control cabin and a sense of familiarity tugged at him. His interest was so intense that it triggered the study habits he'd lived by for so many years, rather than the quiz habits; and the more he concentrated the more the familiarity faded, to be replaced by a need to learn, to discover each dial individually, each effect of the ship's motion as a separate effect.

With a start, he recognized the symptoms and forced himself to relax, to let his eyes wander over the dials without any conscious attempt to interpret them; to let his senses absorb the small cabin and its smells and feels and information.

This was a Kinco Sixty freighter, better known as a K-class, its capacity about half that of the big Earth-Mars freighters. It wasn't a question, it was a fact that he knew.

The circular wall of the tiny control cabin was a checkerboard of insulation squares, except that most of them were covered by instruments. These ships didn't spin to give their crews gravity; thrust was the only gravity they offered. So the river system of hull-shielding which gave Earth ships their spin-gravity could be replaced by compartmentalized shielding in hull sections. The squares would give individual access to the many sections of shielding behind.

The air lock was directly behind Stan and Paulsen as they sat in the acceleration chair-couches that could be lowered nearly to horizontal for high-G thrust. Between the couches and the air lock was the tiny well that gave access to the decks below; and in a small opening built into the wall above the air-lock bulkhead was the emergency medical kit.

The instruments before them were plainly visible from both seats, and the controls were double so that either he or Paulsen could maneuver the ship. Their one-tenth-G acceleration would continue for half the trip and would build them to tremendous velocities on an exponential curve; then they'd start decelerating for the second half of the trip, to come into relative motion with the asteroid that was known as Belt City.

Paulsen could accelerate the doughnut into a Hohmann orbit, then drop it and take them at higher accelerations and decelerations to their destination; but since he was shepherding this load and would probably pick it up himself, the chances were he wouldn't bother. But he could. And that brought up the possibility—the probability—that the *Sassy Lassie* had been one of the ships of the Belt Uprising. Had Paulsen. . . ?

Excitedly Stan turned to the skipper, but his thoughts were cut off by a thunderclap which hammered his body. Instantly the explosion was followed by a high-pitched, whining scream that echoed on each nerve, and the internal feeling of bursting that meant rapidly falling atmospheric pressure.

Terror tore at his nerves—the terror of vacuum, of space, of the emptiness around the tiny ship; of the internal explosion in vacuum that would extinguish forever the tiny spark that was himself . . .

Yet the terror seemed to lie on an unimportant shelf of his consciousness, while his body took on a life of its own—opening his mouth and yelling to expel the pressure from his lungs.

Then his eyes turned as of their own volition to Paulsen, whose lips were moving, whose fingers were reaching out to a control—the control that would cut the motors, Stan realized. At the same moment he found himself releasing the straps on his own body and pushing out of the deep seat, twisting with the push to bring his hands into line with the small opening in the wall above and behind their seats.

The shelved panic jibbered at him as his fingers found the opening and began groping, since his eyes were losing their focus. The scream was fading, then cut off abruptly just as his fingers found the syrettes they were seeking. He grasped two and reached one toward Paulsen.

The skipper was almost beside him now, a hazy figure, and Stan groped for his hand, forcing one of the syrettes into it. Then he brought the remaining syrette to his leg with a slap that forced the needle in and injected its contents into his system.

The jibbering idiot on the shelf of his mind was subsiding slowly as he pulled the syrette carefully out, pinned it to his tunic. His eyes now could barely make out the most gross objects in the cabin swinging lazily about him as he spun slowly in free fall.

The dioxo solution from the syrette spread a warm glow through him. Stan opened his mouth wide and expelled the last of the air that was doing its best to strain out of his lungs. The pressure in his ears let go with a loud pop. The cloudy look of things before him and the burning sensation in his eyes caused him to squeeze them tight shut, and as he did so pain shot through them, and the jibbering panic clawed again for his brain. Tiny crystals of ice were grating across the tender surfaces of his eyes, he knew; and as this was followed by a sensation of cold, he realized that the boiling tears would freeze in the vacuum around him and freeze the eyelids shut.

Something grasped him, and momentarily the panic took over and he twisted ready to slug. Instantly he realized that it was Paulsen, and he took the fear almost physically, shoving it aside and completely away, before he turned his attention back to what Paulsen was doing.

It felt as though he were being stuffed into a bag, but there was no sound. Then he felt drawstrings pull tight at his shoulders and across his chest, and abruptly there was pressure around his face again. And Paulsen was sliding the bag down over his arms, tying it at each joint; then down over the torso with a repeated lacing.

Blinded by tears, Stan opened his eyes to see clear plastic standing only inches ahead; and, as he began to breathe again, Paulsen's voice came to him over a tiny speaker somewhere in the hood.

"That's right, Dustin. Work your jaws and the swallowing mechanisms. Keep blinking your eyes."

As Stan became more aware of his surroundings, he saw that he was in a loosely fitting plastic bag, tightly belted at each joint.

I'll be damned, he thought. *A Mickey Mouse.*

There was a tingling sensation in his throat, and he realized that the "air" he was breathing was not air but carbon dioxide quickly developed from a small plastic pack of acid and soda, from between which the separating plug had been pulled; a gas generator designed to supply the necessary minimum pressure to the suit. It was a device that could not have been used except for the diox which would supply his oxygen requirements for the next hour.

Temporarily safe, the panic vanished to whatever realm he had thrown it, Stan found a handhold and turned himself toward the control panel.

Paulsen was in his seat now, checking the space around the ship for enemy craft—but *the guy wasn't in a spacesuit!*

Unbelieving, Stan stared. Paulsen had on a hood, but just that, over his regular red pilot's suit.

But of course. That pilot's suit *was* a gas-proof spacesuit; and the hood that had obviously been unzipped from a pocket at the back of the pilot's suit collar had a similar low-pressure gas-generator packet.

Stan sighed his relief, then let his attention slide to the deep hole in the checkerboard wall centered above the control panel.

The hole was a full two-foot square that had blown through to the outside of the hull and was now crushed there; a mess of metal and foam plastic insulation, at the bottom of what seemed to be a square tunnel into the hull structure. The water shielding from the compartment had obviously been blown on through into space, followed by the air from the control cabin; but the hole through which they had blown could not be seen past the mess of metal and plastic.

Paulsen was through with his check now, and his face looked puzzled, but he only said, "I'm going to put us under drive to get gravity, then we'll see what the damage is."

The return of even the light one-tenth-G gravity was grateful to Stan's senses, and the cabin reoriented quickly around him.

"If we can work fast," Paulsen's voice came to him abruptly over the tiny intercom, "we can save having to pressurize the bunk area to get you into a tightsuit. I've got plug-in compartments aboard, of course, so it shouldn't take more than half an hour to clear up this mess. Do you think you can take the Mickey Mouse for that long?"

Experimentally, Stan flexed his arm and found that it responded stiffly. The veins that had been standing out like cords against his taut skin were beginning to recede. The rapid breathing induced by the one hundred percent carbon-dioxide atmosphere was exchanging nitrogen out of the blood at a rapid rate, and pressure was equalizing between himself and the suit.

"Seems okay," he said. "A little stiff and a few cramps, but yeah, I can work like my life depended on it. I didn't know they were plug-in compartments, though. I can take the Mickey Mouse all right. I just didn't know the problem could be resolved so quickly."

"It's a Belter, not an Earthie system. You've surprised me so often with your Belter know-how, I guess I'm surprised now when you don't know." Paulsen chuckled, then without another word crawled into the tight tunnel.

It was several minutes, while his squirming legs were the only indication of motion within, before his voice reached Stan again.

"I think I've got it more or less in one piece. Pull me out, but slow and easy."

Stan took hold of Paulsen's ankles, braced himself against the pilot's seat, and started a slow tug, following instructions as he pulled, unable to tell what was going on.

"Harder. Oops. Hold it. All right, pull. Damn it, lost it. Push me back an inch. Not more than an inch."

It only took about ten minutes, but they seemed long. Finally, shoulders pas the edge now, Paulsen pulled his head out. "You can hook on and get it the rest of the way," he said. "My muscles are cramping."

Stan reached his arms, head and shoulders in, and found to his surprise that the walls slanted outward from the opening, to fit the larger squares of the outer hull plating. *Of course,* he thought. *They'd have to.*

He felt around until he got the positioning of the package of crushed metal and foam plastic, found jagged handholds, and began to inch the mess out. When, with a jerk, the wreckage let go its final hold, it dropped him, jagged package in his lap, into the pilot's seat. He sat there a minute, panting, then looked around.

He was alone in the cabin.

For a minute he stared frantically around the small room, and the imp in his mind chanted wildly, *The skipper proved shy, dropped out past the sky; and alone in a ship and in space am I.*

A sudden laugh burst from him.

"I'm bringing up the plug-in unit," the skipper's voice came to him. "What's so funny? You all right?"

"The wreckage fell out and sat me down in the pilot's chair," Stan said.

"Don't touch anything!" was the only answer.

Stan was even more amused. *"Don't touch anything," the man says. I whop back into the pilot's seat, carrying a package that spills onto anything and everything around, that would have knocked anything fragile in spite of me, and he says, "Don't touch anything."*

Then he told himself more soberly, *Well, he's right. I should have been more careful, and I'm right apt to*

send us on a wild orbit to Pluto if I don't get this blasted
package out of the way with a bit more care.

Before he could do much cautious maneuvering,
there was a thump as something was levered up
from the cabin below; and the skipper's voice said,
"Wait." A minute later, Paulsen was at his side,
carefully lifting the wreckage from his lap.

"Stay right there. I'll be back," he said, taking
the wreckage into the freightnut access lock.

Stan relaxed, content to be the inept passenger
for whom the skipper must care. Twisting his head
he could see the plug-in unit Paulsen had brought
—a ten-foot plastic bag filled with water and what
looked like white noodles, sagging against the passenger air-lock, its bottom a point six meter square
of metal and foam plastic. *It looks like a huge boil in the*
bag of noodle soup, Stan decided.

He turned back to the square tunnel before him.
By craning his neck he could see down the two-
meter tunnel to the hull at its far end, and he easily
located the hole by which the water and air had
escaped: a circular hole about six centimeters
across and bulging smoothly outward.

Paulsen had patching material in his hand when
he returned and, Stan estimated, they had about
ten minutes left to do a patching job. Without pausing, Paulsen wriggled into the tunnel and was busy
for several minutes. When he had wriggled back
out, he reached for the plug-in unit, and with Stan's
help fitted it slowly into its niche. When the tip of
the three-meter bag reached the hull, they applied
pressure, squashing it slowly to fit its compartment.
Then, while Stan held the square of inner hull and
cabin insulation in place against the water pressure,
Paulsen snapped its bolts in, and the section was
sound again.

They still had time to spare as the skipper fed air back into the control cabin, though Stan could feel the slightest touches of cramp in his muscles.

"Even lighter pressure this time. We sure been getting rid of the air this trip," Paulsen said over his suit speaker before shucking the hood.

"I'd like to go shares on the air costs, skipper," Stan said, removing his own emergency suit. "It was—"

"Think I can't support my ship?" Paulsen's voice was rough.

"Why, no. I—" Stan clamped his mouth shut, then hastily changed the subject by bringing up what was uppermost in his mind. "That hole didn't look like an accidental rock coming in to me, skipper," he said cautiously. "It looked more like an internal explosion."

The other looked at him queerly. "Yep. It sure wasn't any accident."

"But it was so easy to fix up! No real sweat. Why in hell would anyone bother?"

"That's what I was going to ask *you*," Paulsen told him tartly. "And since we're sharing this trip together, maybe you'd better let me know at least how serious it's likely to get."

"But it's *your* ship. Somebody must have been after *you*."

"I thought of that. I thought maybe the Earthies had started sabotaging Belt ships at Mars. But anybody who set out for a systematic system of sabotage would have taken time to find out how Belt ships are built. It wouldn't have been a hasty, ineffective job like this one. Then I thought maybe you were an Earthie spy, and somebody in the Belt was after you. But in that case, I'd have been in on it. So

either of those is possibly the reason, but not probably."

Stan was silent. Finally Paulsen went on, "On
the face of it, I had a chance. Not much of one, but
a chance. But you didn't.

"Somebody pulled out the plug-in unit and put a
charge—probably detonite—between the bag and
the hull. That somebody didn't know much about
Belt ships because he must have expected the explosion to take the whole hull section out in one
whoosh. If that had happened, the inner wall and
insulation here in the cabin would have gone out
with it, and we'd have died of explosive decom-
pression, even though we were running at low pressure.

"But he used only enough detonite to make a little hole in the hull section, so he didn't know the
hull is built of boron filaments and aluminum—
alfibe. Those hull plates don't break worth a damn;
and when they do break they have a tendency not to
come apart; simply crack along predetermined lines
and stay in place.

"Since there was only a small hole, when the water whooshed out the inner hull plate with its front-
ing of insulation smashed against the hole and kept
the cabin air from going out too fast. Saved our
lives.

"Now, that's part luck," the skipper went on,
"and the guy that did it didn't know Belter ships
very well. But he *did* know sabotage. He knew how
to get in the ship, and he knew how to set a charge.
And he'd allow for a bit of luck on our part. The
rest of my reasoning doesn't depend on luck.

"You're an Earthie. You're an Earthie passenger. You wouldn't have been expected to know

about diox. Even if you knew about it, you wouldn't know where it would be found. Even if I'd been the one to get it and hand the syrette to you, you wouldn't know what to do with it without waiting for instructions, and that would have been too late.

"You're supposed to be dead, Earthie. Which tells me that somebody wants you dead real bad. Which also tells me I'm a sitting duck as long as I'm with you, and maybe you'd better give with a little info."

As Stan stayed silent, the other shrugged, then started to pull the log toward him. His hand hesitated on the book itself, and slowly withdrew. Then he leaned back, clasping his hands behind his head.

"Look," he said conversationally, "I'm not prying. And I'm not asking many questions. And who you are and what you are is not essentially my business. But when a high-G Earthie—"

"A *high-G* Earthie?" Stan asked almost timidly.

The skipper looked at him in disgust. "High-G. With the bucks." At Stan's obvious puzzlement, he went on; "On Earth you have normal gravity. In the Belt, gravity's hard to come by—one of the more valuable commodities. In Belt City, for instance, you live out on the rim, you get full gravity. You pay more freight to live there. Takes real credits to live out on the rim."

"Oh. You mean I'm rich. What an expression. But why—"

The instant flush of anger on Paulsen's face took Stan by complete surprise.

"So I wasn't born on Mother Mudball. Is that—"

"Of no consequence to me, one way or the other," Stan interrupted. "It's quite logical that there would be some differences of expression between us."

"But quaint and Beltish of me to remark on them, I suppose? You Earthies—"

"Oh, can it, Paulsen. I wasn't knocking down on your Belt ancestry. I was asking a question. I came out here to learn things, not to get into arguments over whose parents picked the right place to live."

As suddenly as he had clouded up, Paulsen grinned. "Sorry, pal. I guess I was leading with my chin on that one. But it's unbelievable how overbearing some of you Earthies can be. And when I realized I'd stepped in for you on Mars; and risked my ship—without knowing I was going to—by taking you aboard; and you hadn't warned me word one—and when you ignored my question . . . I'm not prying," he added defiantly, "but by God—"

"You don't have to pry. I'll answer any question you want to ask. I'm as puzzled as you are," Stan admitted. Then he asked, "But why shouldn't you pry? It's your ship, and—"

"I reckon," Paulsen said slowly, "that's another difference between Earthie and Belter. On Earth, everything about you is in the computers, and anybody can find out anything they want to—like what you spent and where you spent it, and probably, if they're interested, why.

"But in the Belt, the only thing anybody else needs to know about you, unless you want to tell 'em, is what job you're doing—which they can tell by the color of your suit; or what kind of training you have—which they can tell by your belt. Those are useful bits of information for you to have other people know. If you don't want 'em known, you change to a plain suit and a plain belt. Inside your belt is your credit rating, which automatically changes as you spend or get credited—but that's private information unless you want to display it; and though it goes through the computer, nobody else can get at your credit rating in the computer but you.

"So a man's not subject to interrogation by computer or by anybody else, unless he wants to be. And it's . . . well, you just don't pry into a man's business. It's *his* business. If it affects you, you stay with him or you leave; but you don't pry."

"Well," said Stan. There was a lifetime of training behind that "well." It was a lifetime habit that anybody could know anything about you at any time, except for the privacy cloak and the immediate moment, and it took time to digest the fact of his obvious freedom from that sort of—yes, prying. Then:

"Would it be prying to ask why you took on the Mars guys when they wanted to arrest me?"

Paulsen leaned back his head and laughed, a loud, long tension-relieving laugh, and Stan found himself smiling in return.

"You can ask, but I don't think I rightly know the answer to that one," he said at last. "I wasn't looking forward to an Earthie passenger, but—well, you got off the ship without a damned privacy cloak. And then there was the belt. Out here a gold belt means A.T. training; and the level of training is indicated by the workings of the belt. I didn't think your belt meant anything, but it . . . well, it might have. Then you walked straight and you talked straight. You didn't sort of *slink* like most Earthies. And anyhow," he added defensively, "Marsers and Earthies—they just aren't *allowed* to interfere with a Belter. We don't let 'em."

Stan thought a minute before answering. Then:

"I don't know why anyone would be after me," he said slowly. "I was as surprised as you were—probably more so—that those guys had a warrant for me from the school. I'm supposed to be home for a two-week leave; and I'm supposed to report back to the school. But it's just a school," he added, and knew himself instantly for a liar. He'd always thought of it as just a school, until the day he'd left. But that—it wasn't something you could explain, even if you wanted to.

"I'd say," Paulsen was speaking in a slow drawl now, "that, if it's the school, they want you back, dead or alive."

"Yeah," said Stan. "It—well, it just *can't* be the school. But it can't be anyone else, either."

"You said I could ask anything I liked. Okay. It may be important. Damned well could be important to you; and it is to me as long as you're aboard. So I ask: What are you doing out here anyhow?"

"I guess I'm running away from the school. They were training me for the military, I just found out. I didn't like the idea."

"Oh? So you just up and ran away? You must be *really* high-G to afford it."

Stan grinned. "I had only enough to get to Earth Orbdock. I was trying to find a job on a ship, when a guy came and said he was my Uncle Trevor's lawyer, and that I'd been left some stock—a thousand shares—in something called Astro Technology. He also left me passage fare out, so . . ."

At the look on the other's face, his voice ran down. What could he have said to cause a reaction like that?

5

The human-information storage, retrieval, and action sequence systems do not have the analytical capability. Information storage is eidetic; action is based on the information stored. When information is introduced in a manner that bypasses evaluation by the intelligence (the dynamic of the interface), it is accepted, stored, and presented for action as of equal validity with other information.

——*Findings in Centric Analysis*
#111264/77

The silence went on and on. Stan waited. Finally Paulsen spoke.

"Your name's Dustin," he said. It wasn't a question. "And your uncle was Trevor Dustin." He looked at Stan in awe. "Do you have any idea who Trevor Dustin was?"

"He—he was nicknamed Trail Duster, I've been told," Stan said. "He was killed in the Belter Uprising. . . ."

"He was the biggest hero of the Belter War of Independence," said Paulsen reprovingly. "He was the guy who—well, he was Mr. Belt. He was the guy who invented ship-guerrilla; who invented ship-freeze. He had us paint our hulls black to radiate the heat out and freeze the hull-shielding water so we didn't blow open when a laser beam bit into the hull. He was the one who invented putting soft plastic noodles into the shielding water to absorb freezing expansion and to take up the hydrostatic shock from those laser hits.

"He was the one invented the carbon-dioxide blow around the ship to confuse the Earthie ladar aiming devices and to absorb most of the strength of the Earthie's carbon dioxide laser beams before they ever hit us. We'd fire liquid carbon dioxide ahead of our ships, and it would make a cloud of carbon dioxide gas orbiting right with us while we fought. He taught us to sting the Earthies with our tails, since we didn't have the firepower to hurt them . . .

"You're *Trail Duster's* nephew?"

Stan nodded dumbly, his mind racing. After years of hearing of "Traitor" Dustin of the Belt Uprising . . .

Paulsen was continuing slowly. "And you've got Trail Duster's shares of A.T.?" At Stan's nod, he went on: "One of his partners is dead; the other's sort of in retirement. A.T.'s in the hands of—well, they're different now. Powerful and power-hungry. They're taking over an awful lot of the policy making out here. A.T.'s different than it used to be but

—but look. This belt." He thumbed the gold belt he wore. "It means I've been trained by A.T.; it's the most valuable possession I own.

"The school's been going down since the partner who ran it went into retirement almost four years ago; but the belt that says you're A.T.-trained will give you top priority on any job they say you've been trained for. It's going downhill, but it's still better than the best."

He looked at Stan again. "If you've got a thousand shares of A.T. stock, I don't have to ask who's trying to kill you. Nor whether it's serious, either. I think the A.T. partner who died—not your uncle; the one who died shortly afterward—well, the scuttlebutt is that he was murdered to get him out of the way of the guys who took over at A.T. It's been hushed, but he probably was. But you're going in the wrong direction. A.T. headquarters is in King sector, about five months from Belt City."

"Five *months?*"

Paulsen laughed this time; a free laugh. "Oh, that's orbital distance, not the time it would take to get there. It's a Beltish system of direction. We use Earth's orbital velocity as the standard of distance for an asteroid—the way you use a clock face as the standard of position for an airplane; or a globe of Earth for the standard of reference in a spaceship.

"For instance, in an airplane—the way it's going would be twelve o'clock. If somebody comes up on it at a ninety-degree on the right, say, above it, that would be three o'clock high. Tells a guy where to look.

"But that wouldn't do you any good in a spaceship. Which way's up? The way you're facing or the way you're going? And are you in an acceleration

couch lying down, or a couch-chair like ours? But—
well, you've got the 3-D Plan Position Indicator. It's
a globe. You use it like a globe of Earth for your
reference."

Paulsen pointed to the global PPI. The faint glow
of orange grid reference lines made it look very
much like a skeletonized globe of Earth. The
navigation stars that the computer selected from the
multitude of stars around them shown as bright yellow dots on the outside surface of the globe. In the
center of the globe was one green spark that represented their own ship. Any outside object, Stan
knew, would be represented by a red spot within
the globe; or if it were a planet or other sizable object, it would intrude as a large red ball. The north-
south axis of the globe was in line with the ship's
axis; north the direction in which they were going,
south the direction from which they were pushed.

"You're in a squadron, diving on the Earthies,
and you want to tell the other ships which one
you're taking. You use latitude—not many of them;
about twenty, forty and sixty degrees of latitude.
Then north and south is like in the scope here;
north is the way you're going. East and west is a
reference from where you're sitting—east is the
right side of the scope from here. Then farside and
nearside, meaning farside of the scope or near. So if
the ship you're after is—well, I don't know how to
describe it except to say 'north forty farside east.'
That would mean ahead of my ship at an angle of
about forty degrees on the far side of my PPI scope
and on an east angle from me. Get it?"

"I think so."

"But an asteroid—well, A.T. is in a position that
puts it in line with a spot on Earth's orbit that's five

months Earth speed further along that orbit than Belt City. So they're five months apart."

"Then you just mean that's its relative position?"

"Yep. Wouldn't take more than two weeks to reach it in this crate. But now, if you want to say where an asteroid is in the Belt, not relative to you in distance, but just where it is, you use the zodiac sign. For instance, Belt City's just entered Taurus; and A.T. is in Libra. Distance is in months; position is in zodiacal sign. Right?"

"Sure. It's easy once you think about it. Makes sense."

"Then there's the other part, the sectors. They're named like a deck of cards—ace, king, queen, jack, ten. The Belt's not evenly spaced around its orbit, you know. It sort of divides up into five sectors, with a fair amount of fairly empty space between. So you've got the sectors to contend with too. Think you can manage?"

"I guess so. *Distance, Earth orbit; position by zodiac. Sector's a card game. Is that what's immediate?*" Stan asked happily.

"By damn," said Paulsen. "Is there anything any time you take serious? Every time somebody starts shooting at you, you spout off some poetry. Where'd you get the poetry habit, anyhow?"

"I never let 'em get said out loud before," Stan said soberly. "But then, there never was anybody shooting at me before. Could that be it? They're my secret vice, you might say."

"Trail Duster was an oddball, too," Paulsen said resignedly, "though I never heard that he made up poetry."

"It's not poetry, it's doggerel. Does my vice bother you?"

"Poetry, doggerel, who cares? You're fast on your feet and you've got an amazing amount of know-how, even if there are some pretty astounding gaps in it that take a guy unexpected. I think I'm on your side, doggy doggerel and all—at least for this part of the action. I haven't liked the way the school's been going recently—the kind of kid they've been turning out. Seemed more like zombies than A.T.-trained experts. I don't know much about the rest of A.T. Enterprises, except they're rooting for war with Earth, which doesn't make sense to me. And maybe if you've got enough Dustin blood in you, you'd be better than what's there now. I damned well better be on your side, at that, if I want to keep my hide, 'cause somebody sure doesn't want you around. So I reckon we better figure how to keep you and me both alive until you can do something with those shares."

"But, what can we do? We're on a ship that they know I'm on, which puts your ship at hazard. And—"

"First thing we do is see if they put a beacon on this crate. Then, when we get debugged, if we're bugged, we put the doughnut on a homing course. . . ."

"Does that mean a Hohmann orbit? It sound as though it should."

Paulsen laughed. "Right. We put it on a Hohmann orbit for Belt City. Then we turn on its beacon and let it coast on in, while we cut loose and get there a bit before they expect you. Can you take four G's?"

"I've never tried, but I assume I can."

"You've taken everything else that's offered. You'll do all right under heavy-G. And I need to strengthen up my bones. Been too long at a tenth, and losing calcium. I'll take calcium, but I reckon you won't need it yet." He paused. "You still want to go to Belt City? Or you want to change course for A.T.'s pebble?"

"I think Belt City. It might be a good idea to find out—"

"Well, at any rate, we'll land there at an unexpectedly early time. You're probably right. A.T.'s a small pebble; you'd be conspicuous. At Belt City, with about six million people around, we can get a bit lost. We'll land at a docker I don't normally use. And once we're docked, we'll skip into the tunnels so fast they won't know where we got to. What do you want to do once you get there?"

"Why . . . I was going to look for a job."

Paulsen stared at him in disbelief, then threw back his head and guffawed. Then, "With a thousand shares of A.T. in his clip, the guy wants to go out and look for a job! Well, well." More soberly he asked, "Do you realize that with those shares you could practically *buy* the Belt? A fair slice of it, anyhow."

Stan's thoughts were chaotic as he began to grasp the implications of what the other had been saying. Finally, "Well, maybe it's . . . What would you do?"

"Actually, I don't know just what I *would* do."

The two sat silent for a minute. Then Stan said, "Maybe I should get a job until I find and speak to somebody who my uncle trusted."

"I know who the retired partner is that ran the school. I think he's even at Belt City. You oughta be able to trust him, I'd think. Lang. Dr. Katsu Lang."

Belt City had originally been a chunk of nickel iron approximately twenty-five kilometers in diameter. In terms of planets, this was practically microscopic; but in terms of the size of particles in the Belt, it was relatively large.

At first it had served as a base for small technological operations, mainly because of its mass. Later it had served those who were interested in the mass itself, and the nickel iron had been carved off in chunks and pieces and carted away; while other chunks and pieces of it had been drilled and bored on the spot to fashion crude reaction vessels for this or that in the line of chemistry.

It was then that Alfibe had taken over; Alfibe Corporation that was using the vacuum of space to draw boron into microscopically thin fibers of tensile strengths far higher than any of the metallic alloys. Boron fiber was not new; it was just that space vacuum made it newly inexpensive to manufacture. On Earth, mass production had brought the costs down from a thousand credits a kilogram to a hundred credits a kilogram. Here the fibers could be drawn for ten microcredits a kilogram— and a kilogram was a lot of fiber.

The boron fiber was a major trade item with Earth, but for use in the Belt it was combined with aluminum from asteroids that were towed in for mining, to create a metal of tensile strength fourteen times stronger than steel, kilogram for kilogram—and a kilogram went a lot further.

So Belt City grew. Port facilities that had been built for the boron fiber trade were enlarged for Belt trade in alfibe; were enlarged again as corporations were formed to build alfibe ships for the Belt.

Where port facilities are available, every form of

manufacture for trade will move in. It wasn't long before the surface of the planetoid, as well as its mined caverns, were crowded.

That was when the Belt City Corporation was formed, its board of directors made up of the heads of the corporations that supported and were supported by the planetoid; its major duty the overseeing of the G-swing, and the balance of industry—in this instance, the *weight* balance of industry.

The terms "gravity" and "G's" were commonly used, but the weight effect was by centrifugal force, and the G-swing necessary to keep that force evenly applied was constantly being upset by new heavy industry moving in; by new construction that failed to take into account the balance and counterbalance necessary to prevent wobbles.

The wobbles were not only upsetting to the manufacture going on, but several times had proved nearly disastrous to the vast hydroponic farms and the "ranches" where meat was grown in vats, the necessary core factors to any Belt habitation; and the swing-weight of the city was shown to be too critical a survival factor to be left longer at hazard to unplanned activity.

The first and gigantically expensive but necessary act of the BC Corp. was the construction of an even flooring over the entire scalloped-looking built-up portion of the planetoid, a section around the equator that extended roughly thirty degrees to the north and south. It was flooring, not ceiling, since centrifugal force applies outward, and the floors of the existing structures were toward space, the ceilings toward the planetary core.

The second and concomitant—and quite as necessary—act was the construction of hull-style river

systems immediately over the floor, similar to the
ones used on Earth spaceships. The rivers were for
inertial control of rotation; huge tanks provided
balance and counterbalance. They also served as
the medium for growth of sea life and plankton as
an additional source of food, and as a far superior
method to the simple hydroponics for recycling air
and waste products.

That was the start of the planned growth of Belt
City; and because of the planning it was now really
possible to grow. New overall floors were needed
and constructed almost immediately, always as a
unit, surfaced with built-in rivers. Transportation
systems for freight and people intertwined through
the growing structures in an orderly and efficient
manner. The internal ecology was protected from
sabotage by unthinking corporate or individual action.

And always, as the city grew, the growing
hydroponics farms moved outward to the rim,
where the plants could take full advantage of the
highest accelerative stress. There were plants that
would grow with practically no gravity; there were
others that wouldn't grow without at least three-
quarters G; but almost all grew best where the gravity was most nearly Earth-like. So the G-swing was
set to maintain full gravity at the rim, leaving the
lower areas to their proportionate weights; and the
plants that were the city's sustenance were given
top priority on that best-growth-potential sector.
Human comfort was never more than a secondary
consideration, though the schools were kept on the
rim, which gave the children full-G during part of
the day; and enough credits could buy you space
between the farms.

Now Belt City hung in space, a wedge-shaped wheel around a central nickel-steel core that was itself caverned and structured for man's use. The floors that made its rim extended now more than twelve kilometers out from the original surface; and where the original sixty degrees at the equator had given the first flooring a width of twelve kilometers, equal to its radius, the outside rim was now nearer twenty-four kilometers across.

From the north and south poles of the planetoid, taking advantage of the null-G at these axes, extended the long strands of bourdon docking and transportation tubes of a space-dock complex. The tubes stretched a good thirty kilometers beyond the nonrotating caps by which they were attached to the rotating asteroid; and each ship that docked was tethered and serviced by several of the tubes.

Fan-powered strutcars traveled the three meter diameter tubes from ship to planetoid cap, then dived across to complimentary tubes in the rotating structure of the planetoid itself.

There were parts of Belt City that gave the impression of being crowded; and there were places where people were likely to be only once a year, or perhaps even less. There were other places where people went only to work. All of the areas were served with air and heat and power and freight and transportation by the tubes and their strutcars that efficiently serviced the entirety of the inside-out asteroid that was Belt City.

Seen from space, the artificialized planetoid looked like a circular deep-sea mollusk, its tendrils of identifying colored translucent plastic highlighted in the unshielded sunlight to make a weaving festoon of yellows and reds and greens and oranges against the black of space.

"The docking tubes look like a man-of-war's tendrils, with the ships its prey," Stan said softly, watching the planetoid enlarge on the *Sassy Lassie's* viewscreen. "Or like a net for invaders."

Paulsen looked at him in surprise. "I reckon they do look a bit like that," he said finally in satisfaction. "The docking tubes are the green ones. The passenger tubes are yellow. The freight tubes are the red ones. And the oranges ones are the smaller tubes in which liquids can be carried without being loaded into jungle gyms."

"Jungle gyms?"

"Boy, as much as I've been educating you, there are still gaps!" Paulsen smiled ruefully. "Tubecars you use on Earth, because that's an induction-repulsion linear motor vacuum system. Pneumocars you have at Orbdocks, where the tubes are air-filled, and the cars can run on battery-powered fans. But pneumocars are built for comfort, and they're a luxury we haven't gotten around to out here. Here we have air-filled tubes and the battery-powered fans; but the cars behind the fans are just . . . well, jungle-gym affairs that you can strap freight into or people can ride sitting on the bars. They have floors and skirts for use in G-fields, but the rest is just a batch of struts. They're formally called strutcars."

Expertly the skipper matched orbits with the asteroid, then maneuvered slowly until the *Lassie* hung at the tips of a ganglion of slender green tubes about half a meter in diameter, netted beside a yellow and three red tubes of about three meters diameter; and an orange tube not more than ten centimeters across. He reached over and flipped a switch marked *magnalock,* activating powerful magnetic coils at various spots on the hull, and with a soft *thump* each of the green tubes reached out and sucked onto the coil-area that matched its codepulse.

"We're docked," he said succinctly. "Now, to airlock us into the passenger and freight systems."

While Paulsen worked over the controls, Stan watched on the screen as the great yellow tube bent slowly and unwillingly, stretched a bit, and then made contact with the magnetic coil around the air lock, its internal pressures resisting every motion, but slowly being overcome by the magnetic attraction between its head and the coils. The action was repeated with one of the red tubes, which was made to seek its own type of pulse-code and fall into place over the access lock that would have led into the *Lassie's* missing freightnut.

"Okay, bud," Paulsen said, unstrapping himself almost as the red tube thumped into place, "here's where we get lost. You think you can fly the tubes, now that you can see how far out we are? Or had we better take a chance on the strutcars. We could go freight—"

"I can fly," said Stan shortly, refusing to notice the tightness in his gut as his eyes traveled the tube to its distant destination. Then noticing Paulsen's quizzical eyes on him, he unstrapped and pushed his way in the null-G toward the freightlock where they'd already prepared their wings and fins.

He was wearing one of Paulsen's bright red pilot's suits now. "You better be in spacemen's outfit," Paulsen had said. "Wear mine until we can get you some of your own." "But they're pilot-red," Stan had objected, "and I'm not a pilot. How do I get to be one?"

"By flying a ship," Paulsen said. "Here, fly this one and do me a few navigation problems." It had been as simple as that. Once he had proved to a competent pilot his ability to fly and navigate a ship, he was entitled to wear pilot-red. His gold belt, though, was his own.

The wing and tail outfits they would wear, flying the tubes, had been blown up in advance, and Stan had practiced getting into them, had been instructed carefully in their use. They hung now in the air lock, ready: two stubby wings, scarcely longer than his arms and shaped somewhat like a bee's wings, coming to nearly nothing at the shoulders but expanding quite broadly in the direction that would be below his hands when his arms were outstretched. A seven-foot tail that would run from his waist to well below his feet, broadening out into a two meter curved arc at the bottom. Wings and tail were of flimsy plastic, stiffened and shaped by blown-up bourdon tubing, like veins. They were attached to straps that ended in a strap around his waist, and the tube for blowing them up was already tucked neatly into its pocket.

In the null-G he had no trouble slipping his feet into the foot-grips about halfway down the length of the tail; belting it to him with the belt that went around his waist, then reaching down and pulling the wing-straps across his shoulders, slipping his hands into the handholds of the wings. Gently and experimentally, he moved a wing and found himself caroming into the air-lock side.

"Save it for the tube," Paulsen said shortly, palming open the air-lock bulkhead before slipping his hand into its own wing-grip.

Before them the tube stretched out, an eerily glowing red diminishing to a point in the far distance; infinitely long, infinitely fragile.

Stan made an involuntary motion and found himself flying into Paulsen, who swung out his arms in counteraction and was propelled out of the air lock into a long glide down the tube.

Stan found his muscles freezing, his gut tighter than before, as he watched Paulsen kick his feet up at the knees, and then snap them down to come to rest spread-eagled across the three-meter-diameter tube, wings and tail touching the sides.

"Watch out for those unintended movements," Paulsen called back. "Did you see the stop I made? Do you get the idea?"

Stan took a deep breath, forcing his muscles to relax. He got his voice under control before he said, "I think so. Every slightest motion sure counts."

"Yep." The other's voice echoed in the tube, but his body was blocking what every sense told Stan was a long fall to the bottom of a steep well. He took the time to get over the panic while he listened. "Tail motion is the most important part," Paulsen's voice was saying. "A gentle up-down swish of the tail with the arms held rigid will give you plenty of speed. The arms can propel, too, if you're in a real hurry. If you want to stop, just flip yourself over like I did, but don't forget to straighten out, or you'll keep right on tumbling. I'm going ahead. You come on along."

With that, Paulsen pulled his wings down toward his body, flipped them, straightened them along his body, and dove off down the tube, tail undulating in a smooth, powerful stroke that had him speeding down the tube like a bird in flight.

Poised on the lip of the air lock, Stan tucked his head down to align it with the direction of flight and slipped his wings open. His head scraped the tunnel, slid along it. He kicked his tail, found himself twisting, and brought his wings into play again. He was moving rapidly, but his head was scraping first one side then the other.

In automatic reflex, he pulled up his feet. The tail flipped over, sending him end-over-end in a wall-to-wall passage down the tunnel. Frantically he pushed his feet out, pinioning his wings. His head buried itself deeply into the soft wall of the tube. He threw his arms and legs wide, and found himself stopped, spread-eagled across the tunnel.

But unhurt.

Dizzy, he looked around. There was the tube, stretching away and away. His wings looked a bloody red in the eerie light. And Paulsen would be far ahead by now.

I'd better catch on and catch up fast, he thought through the dizziness. *But I'm not hurt.* He found his confidence returning.

Carefully he pulled in his wings, gave a light flutter to his tail. He was moving down the tube, but scraping from wall to wall. Experimentally he balanced his wings, flapped them gently. The motion, tried gently, centered him more or less in the tunnel, so long as the tail flapped evenly and slowly. The walls of the tube were moving past at a fair rate, and he was scraping them very little. He increased the motion of his tail. His speed increased violently—and his head rammed firmly into a hard surface.

Summoning every bit of presence of mind he possessed, he flipped his tail, then straightened it, threw out his wings, and landed spread across the tube—facing the closed bulkhead of the *Sassy Lassie's* air lock.

"Damn," he muttered. "I'll never get to Twelfth

and Main this way."

Very cautiously now, Stan fanned himself around one wing, aimed himself down the tube and flapped his wings gently once. It worked. Slowly and smoothly he took off down the tunnel. With care he added a tail motion, but his legs were not quite in unison. His speed increased, but the slightly uneven motion added a vector of steering for which he had to compensate rapidly. He was caroming from side to side, but he found himself compensating with more and more efficiency.

His speed was remarkably high, he noted, as the walls of the tube seemed to wobble past his eratic motion; but he was tiring. It was hard work. He knew that once he got into a good stable glide headed along the center, he could rest; inertia would keep him going. But he was still awkwardly wing and tail-tipping the walls when he heard a shout in the distance.

"Halloo," he answered.

"Junction here. Can you follow me?" The voice was coming much louder now, and by craning his neck, Stan could see the rapidly nearing figure spread across the tunnel.

"Move or I'll run you down!" he shouted.

"Pull up your knees, then straighten out," was the reply, too near.

Stan pulled his knees up, then straightened them violently, and found his head thrust firmly into the plastic wall, while his tail scraped to a rest on the opposite wall. He was breathing heavily, fagged out, and, he admitted to himself, still scared.

"That's how you stop." Paulsen's noncommital voice was only feet away. "You get started like this."

Paulsen drew his wings in across his chest,

ducked his head, and allowed the tail to give him a slight kick forward, snapped the wings open again, and was off down the tunnel.

Stan started to try it, found himself confused, stopped. Suddenly he couldn't remember the first motion. His arms were leaden, his legs aching. And I'm in the middle of a tunnel that's umpty kilometers from either direction, and I can't walk it, he told himself. But he couldn't remember the motions.

Abruptly he let go, relaxed, and let his arms and legs take over. Smoothly his arms flipped; his feet waved gently; the tunnel walls were sliding past him. With relief he let the natural motions replace the forced ones he'd been using; slow motions that didn't demand strength, only gentle undulations that took him faster and faster.

In the near distance, he heard a call: "Right turn. Kick only your right leg when you get here." It was a Y-branch and his turn was not smooth, but the compensations were coming naturally now.

Cautiously he craned his neck and sighted Paulsen not too far ahead. There were tiny lights farther ahead, too, and Stan quit kicking, allowing himself to glide along at a speed he guessed to be in excess of sixty kilometers an hour.

"Stretch your legs apart and slow down."

He stretched his legs as far as he could force them and was rewarded with a fluttering, vibrating sensation from the tailfin, and a simultaneous rapid slowing of his forward motion. The stiffening tube members in the tail had been pulled flat by his action, allowing the plastic to wrinkle and flutter to absorbed energy rapidly.

"Okay. Park. Or are you going to run me down?" came the call.

Stan kicked both legs up and back, and once

more succeeded in ramming his head into the soft plastic wall, but this time he was going too fast. The tail scraped the far wall and snapped open again beyond it, leaving him still sailing down the tunnel, but feet-first, a direction of travel for which the device hadn't been intended. The flexible wings bent and tried to wrap themselves around his arms, buffeting him madly first against one wall and then the other. The tail bent, too, and forced his legs into a crouch position; and then—snap—he was headed down the tunnel head-first again, but with most of his momentum gone. Again he tried to brake, and this time was successful.

"Fanciest stop I've seen yet," Paulsen greeted him.

Stan was about to give a short reply when he looked beyond Paulsen to a large open chamber full of moving tubecars that looked like they'd been stripped for action. Freight was fastened haphazardly into the frameworks.

One of the strutcars—an object sized to fit neatly into the tubes, its three-meter fan covered with a mesh grille, its rear simply a tubular jungle-gym— was heading straight for their tube. The monster fan looked lethal for all its grille-mesh protective covering.

"Look out!" Stan yelled. "That freighter wants in. It's going to try to chase us back up the tube."

Paulsen turned in a leisurely fashion as the huge freighter came to a snarling halt about three meters outside the tube, and hung there buzzing at them like an angry, oversize bee.

"It can't come in while we're here."

"Oh . . . good. Hey, could we reprogram one of those to take us where we want to go?"

"Could. But it wouldn't be a good idea. The dispatcher would be alerted to us. Those things have a tracer on them in case they go wrong and somebody has to come out to correct them. It's easier to hitch a ride on one that's going our way. You think you can handle an open space like this? Fly it, I mean?"

"Should be easier than running into the walls of a tube all the time," Stan answered, "as long as you're sure one of those outsize bees out there won't try to eat me for a rose."

"You haven't got enough oil for that kind of bee to worry about." Paulsen dove gracefully from the tube, and Stan followed. They'd barely cleared its mouth when the big strutcar, with a final angry buzz, dove in and accelerated off in the direction from which they'd come.

This time the fact of flying seemed almost familiar; and to Stan's surprise he managed it with fair ease. Was this one of the familiarities of the molecular training? he wondered. Surely it hadn't been an intentional part—or just possibly it had.

Ahead of him, Paulsen had come to a hovering stop over one of the dark tunnel mouths that led across the planetoid, identifiable only by its code name; and then had settled gracefully onto the very lip of the tunnel, his feet inside its mouth. It seemed odd. To Stan, the tunnel was still overhead; but Paulsen was sitting on it, his feet in it.

Abruptly Stan's senses reoriented. It was a floor from which the tunnels led down, though he knew they actually led out over the surface toward its built-up equatorial section. And, he realized, the circular walls of the entire dome-shaped room would all become floors if you sat on them. Was it the act of sitting? No, he could feel the faintest of tugs that held him to the floor. There was gravity, if only the slightest shadow of it; the gravity of centrifugal force that would pull in all the circular directions around the axis away from that axis.

Paulsen had divested himself of his wings and tail. As he was deflating them, Stan shucked his own wings and settled himself precariously. There wasn't enough G-pull to feel safe, his feet dangling into the dark pit of the tube that stretched away in unilluminated blackness.

The cavern in which he sat was dim, lighted only by the reflected red light of the transparent tubes, now far to one side, through which they had come; and by the faint glow of the signal lamps marking the various tunnel entrances on the curve of floor that stretched in a circle from beneath him, over his head, and back again—the entire circular "floor" would have the same slight tug of gravity away from it, since the tubes all led out from the null-G axis toward the G areas near the equator of the asteroid.

It's unsettling, he thought. *You have to become accustomed to thinking in odd directions.*

The strutcar traffic above him and to his side seemed to be sorting itself out in a haphazard manner, each vehicle searching slowly for the pattern of lights that would satisfy its own equations, then diving into the tunnel that matched its code. The freighters were large and awkward in this space, moving very slowly; and since it would be quite impossible for any one of them to pass another freighter in a tunnel, one of the code signals must indicate whether the tunnel was occupied.

But the other tubes? Stan asked himself. The yellow ones and the orange ones? There was no central column going through this space for the transfer of the contents of the yellow and orange tubes. Obviously, then, this area, where strutcar traffic transferred from nonrotating cap to rotating planetoid, must be the central cap, with other caps around or below it for the other transfers, each with its proper type of junction.

Following Paulsen's lead, Stan folded his deflated wing and tail assembly into a small packet that fitted into a pocket, and fastened it to his belt.

"Why don't we just fly on in?" he asked.

"Ever try flying in a G-field?"

"Well, no. I guess it can't be done. Leonardo da Vinci even failed at that, didn't he?"

"Oh, it has been done. On Mars. Even on Earth. But you need bigger wings and a lot more room to maneuver in. These wings wouldn't hold us up in a tenth of a G. Right here"—Paulsen patted the floor on which he was sitting and almost dislodged himself—"we've got less than a thousandth of a G. But it picks up as you go down—or, rather, across. And from here on we get heavier. I think that's our ride coming now," he added.

Stan looked up at an angry buzzing overhead to see a freighter hovering there, waiting for them to get out of its way.

"This part is tricky. We have to stay in its way until we get in position to jump after it right after it goes by. But don't grab any struts that might pinch you into a wall. These walls aren't plastic. Incidentally, this thing has no sensor circuits on its backside."

Carefully Stan worked his way back in the light-gravity field to just beyond the edge of the tunnel. Paulsen was doing likewise, holding only one hand in front of the big buzzing freighter to bar its passage.

"Let it get all the way in—it'll feel downward

from here—then fall in after it. We'll catch up quick enough." Paulsen pulled his hand out of the way and with a snort of fans the freighter surged forward and dived into the hole. As soon as it had cleared the mouth, Paulsen slid in behind it, feet first, and Stan followed.

Sliding out over the emptiness was like stepping into a soft pillow. He felt as though he were moving downwards, but slowly. It took seconds for the rim to reach his knees, but his momentum was increasing, *per second, per second*, he reminded himself; and his head passed the rim almost rapidly.

It was pitch dark in the tunnel, and for a minute Stan wished that the Belt City Corporation had used the translucent plastic tunnels of the surface— at least until the tubes reached the built-up areas and went inside. Then his eyes began to adjust, and he could see the faint emergency glow from his buttons—the spaceman's last protection against utter darkness in enclosed spaces.

He looked down and could see tiny glowing points that meant that Paulsen was there ahead of him in the pitch black; and beyond Paulsen—near or far, he couldn't tell—the code lights of the freighter. If the freighter had accelerated, as it was quite capable of doing, it would be far ahead of them. Could they catch up? But it would be moving at a steady pace—possibly fairly slowly—and they were accelerating.

By the faint illumination from his buttons he could see the wall of the tube moving gently toward him, and he reached out and pushed himself away. By the feel, he was moving fairly rapidly now. The wall moved toward him again. Coriolis effect? Yes, that would be it. He pushed himself away and found he was falling faster still. The next time it was his back that was scraping the tunnel wall, and as he pushed away again, to fall free, he found his speed quite impressive.

"Look out! Don't land on me!"

Stan looked down quickly. The glowing dots that were Paulsen were moving beneath the code lights on the back of the freighter, and those lights were rising beneath his feet. Slowly at first, then faster; and the illumination they provided gave him a true sense of falling for the first time. Then he was down and onto a package of freight at the back of the strutcar.

"From here on in things get heavier," Paulsen said.

"We're still on the surface, and we're coming away from the axis into the gravity areas. It's about a half-G at the surface at the equator. Then the car will dive on out to whatever level it's dialed to. We'll change to a car for the area we want when we hit the equator shift-space.

"Find a comfortable seat on this side," he went on. "The tubes tilt gradually, so the side of the freighter that drags by coriolis force is the side that has the ground-effect air support; and that's the side that will be dragged by gravity to the bottom when the tube flattens out into a cross-G slant. These cars are designed to go almost everywhere— up, down, or across G. They stay in the tubes, mostly, but they can go out of the tubes for unloading, in half-barrel-shaped runs."

Just when the freighter shifted from fighting the coriolis force that caused it to cling to one wall of the long down-tube, to the fight against the centrifugal force that substituted for gravity here in

Belt City, would have been hard for Stan to say; but now it seemed to be gliding down a less and less steep slope, and slowing as it came to a shift-space between tunnels.

This shift-space was different, Stan realized. It was dimly lighted, and there was a definite gravity. The cars hugged the floor. They crisscrossed their way about the low-ceilinged cavern, searching for new codes, but always gliding only a few centimeters from the floor.

Paulsen was examining a card attached to the package beside him.

"Do we change here?" Stan asked.

"Nope. We're in luck. This one is headed for a shopping area."

The hunting period for their own freighter was brief, and it dove into another tunnel. But this time they weren't falling. The tunnel felt level, and for a while it continued that way. Then they were going downhill again—a sensation, Stan realized, rather than a fact. Actually, they were slanting up-level toward the rim. Now the walls were lighted, and numbers began to flash past; numbers that were blocked out both in the binary code that the strut-cars read, and in common decimal figures. But it was still code as far as Stan could tell, and he felt no familiarity with it.

Occasionally and briefly there would be a widening of the tunnel as the freighter passed a platform level with its own floor, each such dock area causing a *thwop* of changing air pressure as they passed it.

And then they began passing an occasional terminus of a different type; a place in which the car could be halted to shunt sidewise and pass through a lock. Stan was about to ask about the advantage

of this configuration when a surge of deceleration
thrust him forcefully against one of the packages
ahead of him, and the freighter came to a halt next
to just such a system, moved slowly sidewise, and
passed nose-first through a lock.

Immediately beyond the door was a lighted area,
with freighter-troughs leading out between unloading docks. There were two men on one of the docks
unloading a freighter, but most of the docks were
empty.

Their freighter nosed its way into the empty dock
next to the one being unloaded. The men from the
crew straightened and one called over, "Hey,
there."

"Hi," Paulsen answered laconically. "We
hopped a ride in. Our freighter was too loaded, and
we didn't want to wait for a yellow-belly. This is
twelve-thirty-two, forty-seven south fifth, isn't it?"

"Yep. Area one, seventy-five, sixty-third."

Stan felt his stomach wrench. As the man had
straightened to accost them, one had shown himself
to be long and willowy, arms hanging out of proportion to his height; the other to be short and stubby.
He kept from averting his eyes.

"Which way to the walks?" Paulsen was asking.

"Through that door. Shops."

"Thanks."

They went through the door into a walkway;
mall-centered, shop-lined, its ceiling perhaps eighteen meters above them, and five levels of walkway
between their own and the ceiling. The flowered
and shrubbed mall served as the well to the multi-
leveled walkways of the shopping area; and Stan
could see stairs leading from one level to another at
intervals.

His first impression was of color—a riot of color. There was color in the luninescence that flooded from the far ceiling; from below the walkway above his own; from every partition between the shop windows along the walks. There was color in the flowered and shrubbed mall, color in the display windows of the shops, color in the costumes the people on the mall were wearing.

There was an air of gaiety to the scatterings of people around, and the gaiety and color were infectious.

It was several minutes before Stan could sort out individual impressions; and then it was with an empty feeling at the pit of his stomach that he realized that under the color, under the gaiety, something was very wrong. The Mutt and Jeff of the freight docks were not isolated cases, if the people he was seeing were any sample. The willowy, gangling form was predominant; the shorter, squat form less in evidence; but almost everyone, male and female, presented some grotesquerie.

There were burns and scars to be seen. That might be expected of a pioneer society, he thought. But the differences in build and structure of the majority from the norm he was used to . . . It was like a hydroponics farm not properly tended, missing some of the essential elements; or grown without proper light, or with poor G considerations, Stan decided, and knew he had the answer.

There were a few normally formed persons like himself and Paulsen; but they were so far in the minority that he knew himself to be quite conspicuous.

Paulsen was leading them into a restaurant, and as they sat down he didn't wait to be asked. His voice was gruff, held a bitter note of defiance.

"Space is unforgiving," he said, "and the sins of the parents *are* visited upon the children unto the third and fourth generations. Sins of omission and sins of commission," he added. "And ignorance is no defense."

He paused for a minute while his eyes sought through the people at the tables around them and then returned to Stan, who sat silent.

"As a matter of fact, ignorance not only isn't a defense, it's the one unforgiveable sin out here. Unforgiveable by space, that is. Ignorance kills, and it kills right now. Or it maims. Ignorance and stupidity.

"You're seeing the small ignorances and stupidities when you look at the people here at Belt City. Not enough provision for this; not enough attention to that . . . little errors. The big errors—their results are death. Even so, this is a protected environment, here at Belt City. A freak can still stay alive. Outside Belt City, a small error in judgment is sure death.

"You can't be just an average joe and survive in the Belt. You can't let anybody else do your thinking for you and expect to survive. We each live our own lives and do our own thinking out here—and we each pay our own price for our own inabilities. We don't do it because we figure it's a good way to live, to be independent and stay on your toes; but because if you don't, you *don't* live.

"And any one of the joes you see out there—the ones who got metabolically unbalanced and grew beyond their strengths, or the squat ones who got G-squashed, maybe before they were born, or the burned or the deformed—any one of them is still brighter and more able to take care of himself under any circumstances and to do his own thinking and to do it so he gets right answers—any single one of them is a better man than any mollycoddled puppy-dog of an overprotected Earthie, and don't you forget it. If they weren't brighter and more able, they'd be already dead—and the death rate's high. Because space hits you where you hurt if you act ignorant or stupid even for a little while, but it hits to kill if you stay that way.

"Space doesn't forgive," he ended.

Then he changed—expression, manner and voice —and Stan knew that this subject was dropped, now and forever, as far as Paulsen was concerned.

Looking around the room in a casual manner, Paulsen said lightly, "There's a telescreen over there. You go screen Dr. Lang. I'll order us up some rose-hip tea. Then we'll see what gives from here.

The screen was normal Earth-style, and Stan had no trouble with the controls. He kept the screen dark while he dialed computer info for the code for his old friend. Then, as he was about to dial Dr. Lang's number, the screen before him suddenly cleared, and he found himself looking at a heavy face with tiny porcine features. The small, alert eyes riveted his gaze, and the man spoke without pre-amble.

"Mr. Dustin. I am Jonathan Weed of Astro Technology. Your activities since the *Sassy Lassie* docked have been reported to me from no less than five different sources. Your current whereabouts is pinpointed as twelve-thirty-two, forty-seven south fifth; area one, seventy-five, the restaurant at fifty-eighth.

"Your call to Dr. Lang will not be accepted.

Since A.T. is only one of several parties interested in your current activities, and since you must know that your interests lie with A.T., I suggest that it would be to your advantage to report to my office immediately, before your life becomes unduly complicated by others. You are, as I hope I have impressed you, easily monitored in our society.

"I am at thirteen-oh-two, eighty-one north sixth, and any of the area directors will bring you to me. Your friend Paulsen can get you to the area."

Stan started to speak, then changed his mind. As his mouth closed, the man on the screen rose slowly, so that the intricately woven gold belt he wore dominated the screen. His hands went to the belt, and framed it from the sides.

"In the name of the Belt," he said in a voice of authority, "I command you to come. Immediately. Unobtrusively but rapidly."

Abruptly, Stan cut the connection, rising from the seat in the same motion. He turned to see Paulsen standing behind him. He had evidently heard and watched the conversation.

Paulsen was smiling gently.

6

Electronic assimilation of data is fast, but on a bit-per-signal basis, which makes it too complex for storage in the receiving computers, and necessitates biochemical storage in the body and holographic storage in the field. Every look around a room picks up a few hundred thousand bits of data in input information. One estimate is that input data is on the order of ten to fifty million bits per second; and all of this information is retained.

*——Findings in Centric Analysis
#111364/77*

"They've spotted us!" Stan said furiously. "Let's jet."

Paulsen nodded, still smiling, and turned toward the walkway, taking long strides that would appear unhurried but would cover a lot of territory fast.

Stan fell into step with him and continued talking. "The guy said he was Weed at A.T., and that he'd had a tracer on us since we left the *Lassie*, but I doubt that. They simply spotted us when I tried to call Lang. Must have his phone monitored. That Weed character! He was trying to give me some sort of hypnotic command or other to get the hell up to his office. What a dullie!"

Paulsen was leading them back to the freight-loading area behind the shopping center through which they had come, apparently thinking to take the same freightways.

"You going to double back on the same trail?" Stan asked, worrried. "Now they've spotted us, it should be easier to trace us. Maybe—"

"Doesn't matter. Mr. Weed just said to be unob-trusive. I don't think any of the others have spotted us yet."

"Any of the others?"

"He warned you that others were looking for you, too," said Paulsen impatiently. "We're to be unob-trusive about getting to his office, but I don't think we have to hide exactly. It will be just as well if A.T. *can* trace us. Then, if anybody else stops us, they can get to us to help."

Stan came to an abrupt stop, and Paulsen turned to see what had happened. Paulsen's eyes held a strange blankness.

"Where are you taking me?" Stan asked.

"To Weed's office, of course. We're to hurry."

Stan stood stock still, estimating his chances. Without Paulsen he was indeed a stranger in a strange land. But with Paulsen?

Why hadn't it occurred to him that the A.T. school was a molecular memory training school? Katsu Lang had headed each; and each had turned out—robots. If he had needed any demonstration of what Mallard had been talking about, he had it now before him.

But why wasn't he himself reacting in the same manner as Paulsen? The command had been "in the name of the Belt." And it was quite obviously a phrase that keyed in a hypnotic condition. But there'd be another command phrase for use on Earth, and that hadn't been used. Okay, he was safe until somebody started using whatever phrase had been selected to key in his own robotic responses. He shivered violently, knowing his own vulnerability to be as great as the one he was witnessing. Then, with an effort, he pulled himself back to the immediate problem.

He and Paulsen were facing each other just inside the door to the unloading area. From the corner of his eye, Stan could see the Mutt-and-Jeff freight loaders straightening, beginning to pay attention to what must seem a disagreement—a disagreement in which they would take the part of the Belter against an Earthie.

I'd better make it good, and I'd better make it fast, he told himself.

Idly he let his fingers go to his belt, then glanced down at it. Paulsen's eyes followed his own. When he was sure that Paulsen was looking directly at his belt, he said softly, "Wait here." He started to use the command phrase that Porky had used, but stopped. If he got it wrong, he'd trigger the wrong reaction. Anyhow, it was not a phrase he could bring himself to utter.

Paulsen was looking confused. "We are to hurry," he said.

"Wait here. Then we'll hurry."

Not daring to pause any longer, Stan turned on his heel and went back through the door onto the walk. Turning away from the direction of the restaurant, he lengthened his stride toward the nearest byway.

Behind him he could hear light running footsteps. Obviously not far behind, or he couldn't have distinguished them among the numbers of people about. He was just meters away from a byway, but the runner was not many more meters behind.

Abruptly, he turned into the byway. No sooner had he made the corner than he flattened his back against the wall of the shop he had rounded, hands loose and ready.

As the figure came around the corner at top speed, he reached, reflexed, half hit her on the withdraw, and ended up supporting his quarry to keep her from falling.

He was looking down into a pretty Oriental face, topped with mussed dark hair, flushed from running, and completely startled so that the mouth was still open in an O. She was wearing a gold belt over tunic and trousers.

In spite of himself, Stan began to smile. "Every day in every way," he said happily, "the robots get prettier and prettier."

The flush that mounted her cheeks this time was not from running. She pulled away from him in fury, then softened again.

"You're Star Duster," she said breathlessly, "and you've got to trust me quickly, because I can get you out of here. I'm Sandra Lang. Will you trust me?"

"Yes," said Stan, surprising himself. He could rationalize later that he couldn't get out by himself, that trusting her was the best gamble available. There would be all sorts of reasons; but when it came right down to it, he trusted her because he trusted her. It was that simple.

She nodded at him, but remained still, thinking. "They'll have all the strutcars monitored, so we can't go by car," she said hesitantly. "Freight cars, too . . . oh, I know."

Back onto the mall she led him, down a way, across the mall, into a foodstore. Through the store to the back, through a door to the delivery area, looking in every direction, then breaking into a run to catch a man stooping over some newly unloaded vegetables on a platform.

"Mr. Jim." She stopped beside him, panting. "Are you returning anything to the rim right now?"

The face that turned up to hers was graying, lined, a bit grim, but the expression softened as he looked up. "What sort of trouble you in today, Sandra? I thought you'd outgrown hide-and-seek."

"This one's for real, Mr. Jim," she said solemnly. "This is Star. We both need to get out to Gramps, fast and inconspicuouslike."

"Those crates over there," he said, smiling at her fondly. "They're going out to Rosie's. You get in them and I'll dial you to Katsu, then you tell him to dial them on to her. Hop in. How serious if you're caught?"

"Plenty." She didn't amplify the statement, but her tone left no doubt.

"Don't get yourself mixed up in politics, Sandra," he told her severely as he opened two of the biggest crates for them to climb in. "It's not a game for sweet youngsters like you. A pretty face is no protection when it's power politics that's being played," he went on as he replaced the covers and checked the lashings to the strutcar. "And they're playing it rougher every day." Then; "Here you go," he ended, and Stan felt the strutcar begin to move as he lay curled in the dark in a crate on a freightcar near a pretty girl who was the granddaughter, obviously, of the man who had made him a robot. *And perhaps I'm a fool,* he told himself, but there was something inside that refused to believe the statement.

Katsu Lang sat at the keyboard of the symphony master, taking out the tensions that had been building within him in thunderous, rolling tones of barbaric style, harnessed to an insistent violin concerto theme. The contrasting elements delighted him, and took his attention from the chase he knew to be going on, matching the demanding insistence of a violin *rampant,* he thought, to the overpowering brutality of a cadenced base viol clawing at the understructure of the racing theme. The two musical forces were harmonized by a patterned form that included within itself the warring elements—and he found himself quite satisfied with the resultant dynamic stability.

He had turned on the recorder, and he knew that the tensions had given him a body of music which, with a few months spent in organization and handling, could be made into a great work.

With care he brought the two musical forces into a clashing crescendo in which they opposed and then interwove in intricate patterns that shifted from major to minor, until the two flowed together finally in an harmonious whole which at the last instant slid into a triumphant major chord.

Lifting his fingers from the keys, he leaned back in the maestro's great seat and flipped on the recording of what he had just played. It washed over him in rolls of movement and countermovement, and it almost drowned the tiny wrist receiver that told him that Sandra, at least, was back. And young Star Dustin must be with her, he decided, for if she had lost him she would not return until she found where he was taken and what could be done—and that would necessarily have required more time.

Have I written Sandra and young Dustin into my violin concerto? he wondered—matching them against the violent forces of space and man in space that pattern them and are patterned by them into a —hopefully—harmonious score? And knew that he had done just that—had written his hopes and his goals into the music that had seemed to come unbidden to his fingers as he played analyst to the forces involved.

Muting the recorder, he rose to meet his guests, approaching now through the apple orchard beyond the bays of the music stall. The grass carpeting beneath his feet felt resilient; the glow of late afternoon filled the air. He wondered idly if the Earth boy would recognize the programming which kept the light of the enclosure that was his home tuned to the Earth-light sequence for any time of day. Or the need for that programming; the changing colors within the atmosphere modulating a changing of body reactions, preventing the hypnosis that is a single-light-frequency response.

We have so much to learn of artificialized living, he thought; *and,* he added to himself, *so much to learn of learning itself.*

The two coming through the orchard made a graceful contrast to the stubby-fingered grace of the trees, now in full leaf with tiny apples budding.

Paulsen was not with them. It had been some years now since he had seen Paulsen—one of the hopefuls of the program that had turned out to be so flawed. Sandra was light and graceful beside the tall figure of the now-grown man who was Star Dustin. The young man's stride was easy, his head high, the hair a deep flame beneath the trees. He was graceless in contrast to Sandra, but his stride held a strength that was a grace of its own. *How very like Trevor,* Lang thought.

He watched the boy's face as he stepped through the bay into the music stall; watched his slight catch of breath as he noticed that the grass over which he had been walking continued as carpeting of the stall; watched his glance as it went to the acoustically designed canopy.

Then the boy's eyes met his own, and he felt the warmth of pleasure with which the other responded; and, like a slap in the face, the fear and fury which shuttered it almost instantly afterward.

He bowed his head in reaction to the mental blow, then managed to make the gesture into one of greeting.

"Welcome, Stan Dustin, son of my late partner and very true friend," he said formally.

"Son?" Stan's voice was startled, and there was hope behind it.

"You are Trevor Dustin's son, Stan. The other was a fiction of convenience, and in the Belt such fictions are not necessary."

"Then—if I am the son of your true friend—why did you let them make me into a robot?" The words seemed torn from Stan, but he looked straight into the older man's eyes as they poured forth.

"Stan, Stan. Would I have made my own granddaughter into a robot?" The Mentor's voice held a deep distress. "It was a flaw in the system that we did not foresee; that none of our tests had predicted.

And it was a flaw that the people who took over our school—the ones who killed the other of our partners after Trevor died, and who forced me to retire —it was a flaw that they are using and reinforcing."

Stan's face crumpled from the fierce anger it had held, and the hope and pleasure returned slowly to it.

Holding the younger man's eyes with his own, Katsu Lang continued softly, "It is my hope that you will work with me, as Sandra has, and that we can find the key to changing the responses from those of a robot to those of a man."

The work began the next morning. It was based on tests in a cubicle like the one in which Stan had spent so many hours for so many years on Earth.

Between the tests were long conferences with the Mentor, in which they went over each step of the processes he had gone through on Earth.

Stan threw himself into the tests with a fierce exultant hope that was overriden only by the need to eat and sleep. Yet even the sleep was exultant, still with its alternating pattern rhythms; but shot through with three knowledges: that he was the son of Trevor Dustin, that he was in Belt City, and that a solution would be found to the hypnotic control that he had seen in Paulsen and feared desperately in himself.

At the end of the third day, Katsu Lang came to call him from the cubicle into a small study, where Sandra served them tea.

The older man waited until the tea was served and the three were relaxed in deep pneumochairs. Then he said slowly:

"I do not understand what I have found in you, Stan, but the findings are unmistakable. You have taken the same training as the others, and as Sandra has taken. But only you show no reaction whatever to the stimulus-response mechanisms by which it has been shown that the inoculated knowledges are brought forth."

"You mean I'm not a robot?"

Lang smiled gently. "I mean exactly that."

The sentence hung there between them for a long minute, Stan not daring to let himself believe.

"I do not understand, sir. I was trained with the others. I saw Paulsen's reaction . . ."

"Nor do I completely understand. But I have given you every test of which I can think. I have used every hypnotic command I know that has been trained into those who attended either the Earth school or the one in the Belt.

"Then, in case I had not known the ones to which you might be keyed, I have tested your reactions to the information patterns to which you were trained molecularly. And even to these, you responded as you yourself would respond—not as the donor of the molecular knowledge would have responded. You use the material as a young man would use it, armed with vital knowledge from many fields—not as the person would use it who had spent a lifetime acquiring the one set of knowledges, with his reactions shaped by that knowledge alone, and with the thought habits of such specialization."

The relief that flooded Stan's being was almost tangible. Yet there was a tiny doubt that lingered; a fear. He shoved it aside and let the relief burgeon. But then:

"How could I have been the one who was different?" he asked. "I wasn't even as bright as the others. My I.Q. barely measured up to the school's standards."

The Mentor looked at him fondly. "Survival instinct, perhaps," he said. "It has little to do with I.Q. as we know it—but then, we know so little. And our measurements reflect that lack of knowledge."

Then he leaned back and half-closed his eyes. "Actually, I don't know," he said. "You were evidently restudying every knowledge with which you were inoculated on your own, and from your own very different point of view. You restudied the information. You brought it up and looked at it and added in what you found for yourself, and put it back—over and over again, reanalyzed to your own specifications. The answer must lie in that.

"But it must lie, too, in that odd sleep cycle you developed. The 'alternating-current' sleep cycle.

"During the day there is a slight separation of electric potential between the feet and the head. It's caused by the upright position of the body in respect to the Earth's electrical potential. It increases the activity in the cerebral areas. In sleep, the body is placed flat with respect to the electrical potential, and across the field. This decreases the cerebral activity and increases the biochemical and field potentials.

"We learned some years ago that a small electric differential between the core of Belt City and its rim, so that a current flow is created, is a necessity. The magnetic flux follows the same pattern as that for a planet, since the current flow follows this pattern. Perhaps, if we reinforced this . . .

"I expect that in that alternating current sleep cycle you developed a second system for bringing up and amalgamating information in the files; resettling it; fitting it together.

"I don't know. But if we use the same systems

that you used, perhaps we will achieve the same results?"

"But—Dr. Land . . . I *wanted* to study more of what I had learned." Stan paused. "It was more than just a want," he said slowly. "It was like . . . like my sanity depended on it. Like I *had* to do some learning on my own."

The Mentor smiled. "Your survival instinct seems to be more developed than most," he said. "Quite evidently it was necessary to your survival as a rational human being. But I think," he added, "that you got more than you actually bargained for. There are indications that you were dragging up and reviewing not only the informations inoculated into you, but deep knowledges, either genetically or otherwise acquired from way back. Those came up, too. So I think it must have been quite a demand that you put on yourself to know what you needed to know.

"For instance," he went on, looking at Stan quizzically, "when you flew the tubes. Your reactions, I gather, were structured in an accurate, detailed, seat-of-the-pants knowledge of small-plane flying; of flying of a type that hasn't been done since the early twentieth century."

Stan broke in excitedly. "You're right, you know. I could almost feel the flimsy structure of a—a flying machine around me; and a sort of stick in my hands with which to guide her, and someone shooting at me. . . ."

"So detailed? I had wondered. Yes, I think it is undeniable that in pulling up material you had just received, you pulled up material from lifetimes back as well.

"And if that is so, then we have millennia of information waiting to be culled."

The two had almost forgotten Sandra, sitting quietly in a deep chair in a corner. Now, suddenly, she was on her feet, standing before them.

"I wish," she said, "that I had had as much sense as you, Star. But—if I begin now? If I study like mad? If I . . ."

Her voice ran down, and she stood there, tiny, the eagerness in her a vitality of emotion that was sending tears coursing down her cheeks.

"Show me how, Star!" she cried. "I'll work like I've never worked before. I'll—"

Stan rose slowly and came over to her; stood looking down into her eyes bright with the unheeded tears. "It's easy," he said softly. "Or rather, it's not easy, but—when it's something you have to do, deep inside *have* to do, then you can't not. Like breathing," he said. "You just can't not. I'm not making myself very clear, am I?" he asked.

"I'll learn," was all she answered, looking up at him, hope in her eyes.

Stan turned to the Mentor. "And the others?" he asked. "Paulsen and the others?"

Lang nodded slowly. "We'll have to find a way to get them here and put them to work. That's the first problem. Then we'll see if they are capable of the need to know."

Stan smiled. "We've got one advantage in the gold-belters, sir," he said. "That 'need to know' was part of the philosophy of every man from whom the information they received was taken. You don't make an expert in any field unless and until he has that need to know. I think that's the part I happened to settle on first, and that helped to drive me.

"So if we can tap into that part, the rest should be easy."

But in the far back part of his mind, the fear still lurked. Fear that he might not—yet—have won his freedom completely.

Freedom and fear, he thought. *Are they always together?*

7

The information filing systems are about one-third slower than the electronic input and analytical systems. Although filing is a constant, its slower progress necessitates the sleep cycle. During sleep, the electronic input systems are slowed, while the filing systems catch up with the information readied for storage. When sleep is too long neglected, the "ready" files clog, information is lost, and the human configuration slows in its reactions to its environment.

——Findings in Centric Analysis
#111464/77

Stan walked into Weed's office with his head held deliberately high, his shoulders squared, as though the trepidation that might be expected of a younger man faced with the awe-inspiring might of the A.T. Corporation was forcing a defiant reaction.

He held the pose as Weed slowly rose from his seat and extended his hand, which Stan ignored.

"Ah," said Weed, "I see that you are unconvinced, though sensibly coming to see what A.T. has to offer."

Stan nodded curtly.

"Very sensible of you." The porcine-faced man before him nodded his head solemnly. "Very sensible, though somewhat insensitive to retain this obviously recalcitrant attitude. However . . ."

Weed reached into a drawer, pulled out a large signet ring, placed it deliberately on his finger, and stood twisting it, watching Stan to be sure that the younger man had fixed his attention upon the ring. Then, in a voice of command, he said: "I, the trainer, speak. You obey."

Stan felt the slight tug at his senses that recognized the old command, discarded it instantly, and then forced his eyes to take on a glassy stare, his shoulders to slump slightly, his head to lose its defiant lift.

"Ah!" said Weed, and the sound carried a world of satisfaction.

Stan stood immobile, waiting. This was going to be quite tricky, he realized.

"Now, young man, "Weed was saying, "we will get to the business at hand. I made a mistake earlier in not using the correct symbolism, but then I had two of you to control. Hereafter," he went on, "you will respond either to the Earth command I have just used, or to the phrase, 'In the name of the Belt, I command you.' Do you understand?"

Stan nodded slowly.

"Then tell me," said Weed, "to what you must respond, and what response you must make."

"I must respond either to the ring or to the belt, and I must respond with complete obedience," Stan said, keeping his voice flat.

The other looked at him sharply. *Oh-oh,* thought Stan. *I should have said to the phrases backed by the objects. Have I been caught out?* But he maintained his glassy-eyed stare, and it seemed to satisfy Weed.

"Now, young man," Weed said slowly, "I must have your shares in Astro Technology."

Stan let his hand move as though toward a pocket, then hesitate, as though a stronger force were working on him; then move again to the pocket and hesitate again. Finally, he let his hand rest immobile halfway between his pocket and its former position by his side.

"Oh?" Weed was puzzled for a moment. "I gather the shares of stock you possess hold an attraction nearly as strong as the command under which you respond to me." There was silence and he finally added, "Answer."

"Yes, sir. They do."

Weed sank back in his chair and waited a moment. Finally he said, "Give the shares to me."

Stan made the gestures of trying to obey again, again let his hand rest immobile in a halfway gesture and stood silent.

"Why do you not give them to me?" asked Weed.

"I cannot, sir. They were given to me in trust."

"Um." Then, "I could have them taken from you forcibly."

"You could, sir. That would break my conditioning. Then I could fight you." The voice was still a monotone, and Stan waited, forcing his eyes to remain unwavering. This was the crucial point. Would Weed believe that Stan could produce this much independent reasoning, while still under control? Lang had thought he would. Weed was not a fighter; he was a weasler. He would have to figure

this one out, but if he figured it out in terms that
were normal to him . . .

"I was told that you were independent. How-
ever," Weed said softly, "let us reason together."
Stan kept himself from breathing a sigh of relief.
The pig was going to go along with it.

"The shares—the trust—are, I gather, from your
uncle?"

"Yes, sir."

"And what would your uncle's wishes in the matter be?"

"I am not sure, sir. It is a trust. It is a trust to see
that his projects at A.T. are finished in the way in
which he intended them."

"Ah!" Weed began to relax now. He'd been giv-
en a bargaining point, and bargaining was something in which he felt secure. Lang had emphasized
this. *Once you can get him to bargaining, you're on much
safer ground because he will feel safe.*

"And just what were his projects?" Weed was
asking almost happily.

"That the Belt become and remain independent,
sir."

"It is. And A.T. is seeing to it that it will remain
independent. If that is all, you may sign over your
shares to me."

"That I could not do, sir. I was given them in
trust. I might be able to give you proxies."

"Very well. I shall have them drawn up."

"No, sir."

"No?"

"No. The independence of the belt was not my
uncle's only project. I must carry out his projects."

"What, then, were the others?"

"That A.T. remain technologically advanced
over Earth."

Weed's voice lost some of its aplomb. "That's being done, son," he said impatiently. "If you want proof . . ."

"Your word is sufficient, sir."

"Then you have my word. That is being done. Anything else?"

Now, thought Stan. *"Get at least two agreements first,"* Lang had instructed. *"Then—and not till then—bring up the one on which you really want agreement."*

"That the colony on Jupiter's moon be established," he said aloud.

"That is being—" Suddenly Weed paused. This was too easily checked, and the boy had mentioned that the "trust" under which he'd been placed was sufficient to break his conditioning if it were forcibly thwarted.

Weed leaned back in his chair.

The name *Dustin* was one to conjure by in the Belt. If there were a way to get the boy's wholehearted—at least apparently wholehearted—cooperation, half of A.T.'s troubles with the Belters would be over.

The Jupiter colony ship, the *Phoenix,* was a useless hulk; and perhaps this would be a method by which he could get the youngster's open cooperation—as well as getting him out of the way. It would take some cash and time to get the old hulk actually out into the system with Stan aboard, but the time could be utilized for propagandizing the Dustin reassociation with A.T.; and the expense would not be too great.

A smile crept over his features. The boy had unwittingly handed him an ace with which to trump his opponents.

"Your uncle wanted you to see to it personally

that these projects were properly carried out?" he asked, carefully keeping the excitement out of his voice.

Stan nodded.

"And you recognize that the first two have been implemented in the proper manner?

"Then," he said carefully, "why don't I assign you as, say, a vice-president of A.T., to take the Phoenix and carry out the project of the Jupiter moon? Between your A.T. training and your uncle's heritage, you should have the ability necessary."

Stan kept his voice dead with an effort. "Yes, sir."

"Do you know what the *Phoenix* is?"

"She's a ramjet scoop ship, sir, that was readied to pirate air from Jupiter and to ferry personnel to Io to prepare the colony site, sir."

"That's right. She was to prepare the colony site on the moon of Jupiter—Io—and to provide it with atmosphere from Jupiter. Do you think you can handle the project?"

Stan nodded.

"Very well. We will make you vice-president in charge of the Jupiter project, and commander of the *Phoenix*. And for your part, you will sign over those shares to me."

"No, sir."

Weed's face fell. His voice showed the short leash on which his temper was held.

"What now?" he asked with restrained fury.

"The *Phoenix* will have to be rehabilitated. I will have to have a crew, and they must be trained. Then I can give you the proxies of which I spoke."

Weed leaned forward grimly, then relaxed back

in his seat. It was a perfect plan; and obviously, except for this strong loyalty compulsion, the boy was under control.

Well, he could have an "accident" anytime that he went out of control, once it was publicly established that he was enthusiastically with A.T. The expense would be justified. They would actually save money by buying the loyalty of the Belters at the price of refurbishing the old hulk. And the boy might even get the project far enough underway so that it became commercially feasible as a corporate project, in the long run, after the coming war was over.

"Very well," he said. "You will announce your loyalty to the A.T. Corporation as now set up, and will proclaim it widely and frequently."

He watched the boy closely for reaction, but the glassy stare and the solemn nod were his only answer. "We will refurbish the *Phoenix*. It may take several months, and I shall demand your complete cooperation during that time."

Stan nodded again, and again in the flat voice said, "I will pick my crew immediately, and set up quarters for training them. I will announce my loyalty to A.T. as now set up. I will continue to announce that loyalty during the period while the *Phoenix* is being refurbished properly, and while I am training my crew. I will inspect the *Phoenix* occasionally. When we are ready to take off, I will sign proxies for my shares to cover the time in which I shall be absent."

Weed nodded to himself. Not a bad bargain at that, he decided. And if it began to go sour, that "accident" could occur. . . .

Tobey Olsen had started work at the Ace Sector

Ship Yards of A.T. the day that the hunk of ungainly nickel-iron asteroid that was to become the *Phoenix* was towed into the yards.

He'd been cable jumper during the laser-milling of the eight-point-five-kilometer asteroid, when they put her into a free fall spin and milled her just as though she were in a lathe. He'd listened to the jokes about Trail Duster's Folly, and he'd laughed with the crews; but he'd believed in the hulk, and it had been pure magic to him, seeing the rounded, wad-cutter bullet form take shape.

They couldn't do *this* on Earth, he had exulted to himself, watching the jutting crags and the jagged irregularities cut smooth by the knifing of the huge laser beams as the hulk rolled gently and smoothly in the "jaws" of its inertial lathe, and the steel-strong, smooth squat form of the hulk that was to be a scoop ship began to seem strangely akin to his own squat form.

Squat but powerful. The changing Gs that his mother had met while she carried him had formed his own body—smooth, blunt, and powerful—as the lasers were forming the shining irregular chunk of nickel iron before him. The squashing he had undergone had not squandered the strength inherent in his structure, any more than the lasers were squandering the strength of the asteroid they milled so delicately. *We both came out better for the treatment,* he told himself, and to him the *Phoenix* became the symbol of all that was powerful, though misshapen by Earth standards, in the Belt.

By the time the *Phoenix* hull was formed and the milling began that would make nests for 144 K-class ships at her back—the power structure for the bullet—Tobey had been made foreman of a small crew, doing part of that milling. The wafflelike structure that would nest the K-classes was to him the epitome of beauty; a powerful nesting that would give the *Phoenix* a 144-ship boost into high acceleration. The ships would cut loose just before they hit Jupiter's atmosphere, would cut around, and would catch her on the far side, nesting in again to take the scoop ship on to Io.

The tanks that went into the otherwise solid metal of the nose area, and the plugs that would open or close those tanks, were the work of other men; but the tanks were small in diameter and deep in length, and the delicate job of milling the interconnecting tubing from tank to tank was Tobey's; for by then he was one of the most skilled laser-lathemen of the Belt. During the building of the long corridors, cabins, common rooms and life-support systems that filled the *Phoenix* backsides, Tobey was crewmaster.

It was when the *Phoenix* was almost finished that Trail Duster had made him supervisor of the project. It had been a proud day; but less than a week later, he and the crew had been called off.

"The *Phoenix* has got to wait," the red-headed director of A.T. had told him. "Earth is interdicting the rest of the system to Belters. We've got us a war to fight."

Instead, he'd been supervising the reworking of every K-class that could be called in—the 144 scheduled to power the *Phoenix,* along with most of the privately owned ships of the Belt. There had been little time and great fervor, and he'd worked the crews until they dropped, given them a bit of rest, and started them back on the job again.

It was when he had said "ready," that Trevor had said "go," and the Belter War of Independence had been underway.

Things had changed then, with Trevor Dustin dead. Things had changed and stayed changed; and the old *Phoenix* had drifted there in the yards, thirty kilometers from the nearest ship, a sort of stationary anchor point that defined one back corner of the yard—too big to move, and too tied up in corporate policy to use; a vast, monumental junkpile, according to the new powers-that-be at the Ace Shipyards of Astro Technology.

Now Tobey stared from the orders in his hand to the man who had brought the orders to him.

"You're Star Duster," he said fiercely. "I heard you'd gone all-out for the new A.T. setup."

"Yep," said Stan. "I reckoned you'd heard."

"And you're going to refurbish the *Phoenix?* Finish her?"

"Yep," said Stan. "I reckoned you might have heard that too."

"Okay." Tobey's voice was far from friendly. "I'll get a foreman and a crew together. How fast a job you planning?"

"A couple of months. Maybe three."

Tobey whistled. "Well," he said slowly, "she was nigh onto finished when we dropped her. We might could. Where you going to get the K-class? One hundred forty-four of them?" he asked, his voice soft—not dangerous, just soft.

"Don't reckon we'll get more than fourteen," Stan said, and waited.

"Humph," said Tobey and stayed silent. Then; "You won't boost her very fast with fourteen," he said cruelly. "I'll get on her, Mr. Dustin." He turned to the door of her small office, opened it, then flung back over his shoulder, "You sure are trying on big britches for an Earthie."

"I sure am trying on big britches for the son of a

Belter," Stan said softly.

Tobey stood with his hand on the door for a long minute, then turned slowly back into the office and closed the door softly behind him. He came to stand beside the slender red-haired figure seated in the chair beside his desk; his powerful hands hanging limp at his sides.

"I haven't given you a fair shake, have I?" he asked.

"No," said Stan. "I didn't really expect you to, but I was hoping." Then he added, "I guess you're giving me a fair shake now. Will you talk a minute?"

Tobey nodded and seated himself at his desk. "Trail Duster was . . . well, he was Mr. Belt. And I guess I didn't like it when they called you 'Star Duster.' "

"That was the propaganda machine at A.T.," said Stan. "I gotta let them keep it up, too."

"Gotta?"

"Gotta. If we want . . . Tobey, let's start out by scotching some of the rumors you've heard. Not the propaganda. You can scotch that or not as you like. It's a machine product and most buy it, but some don't. I don't think you buy it. But the rumors— that's something else again.

"All right. Rumor number one: The *Phoenix* is a rich boy's play-toy. That one's true. If I weren't rich, I certainly couldn't have it. Trevor made me rich by giving me his shares in A.T. But the *Phoenix* is going to be used. Not just as a base here, or for scooting around the Belt having fun, but to go out and do the job she was intended to do. As soon as you can get her outfitted, we'll be taking off for Jupiter; and we'll be taking a complement of science personnel with us. If you find that you can go along with an idea like that, I'd be glad to have you aboard."

"Not with fourteen K-class for power, you're not going to do the job. Takes a hundred forty-four K-class to boost the *Phoenix* at three-G drive. Fourteen K-class would give you about one-point-three G drive." Tobey paused, then went on bitterly, "And them ain't Earth G's. They're space G's, and you read them 'point three meters per second per second.'"

"Couldn't do it with that, hunh? Yes, I know we couldn't. However, we *could* run a scoop operation that way if we took our bloody time about it. It's velocity that counts around Jupiter, not necessarily drive thrust. If we wanted to take, say, a hundred and thirteen hours to build her up to speed, and another hundred and thirteen to slow her down, and take a chance that our aiming was just right, we could do a dive with fourteen K-class." He watched Tobey narrowly.

Tobey nodded, his expression still hard. "You could," he said coldly. "That what you're planning?" Then he went on without waiting for an answer: "You're right that speed's the important thing. And you figured that time just like out of an Earthie textbook. But you got to do better'n that. There are a few other vectors to add in. Like original velocity, old Jupe's orbital speed, and whether or not you want to come to a complete stop relative to whatever you pick out to come to a complete stop relative *to*."

Stan grinned to himself while he kept his face stern. The guy was hopping mad now, but at least he was listening. "And if I planned to do it that way, then that's how I'd figure," he said. "However, I was only pointing out that it would be possible, so I made the figures more or less arbitrary. From the pragmatic point of view, I *don't* think that's a possible method, because I'm quite sure that A.T. won't play ball."

He paused to let that sink in, then went on: "I figure on getting fourteen K-class, all right—and that's all I figure on. But I don't figure on keeping even those fourteen because I expect that the powers at A.T. plan to let those K's boost me into a Hohmann orbit, and then they plan to yank them back. All of them. On that schedule, if they figure a true Hohmann orbit, I should get to Jupiter in about six years, and, if I do, I could consider that I was a lucky son of a—a Belter. One way or another, though, that would serve A.T.'s purpose and get me out of their hair quite effectively for a bit—wouldn't you think?"

Stan eyed Tobey speculatively. "And now," he continued coldly, "I have just put my life in your hands."

Tobey's face was slowly losing its hard lines as he chewed the problem over before answering. Then a grin began to creep out and his eyes began to twinkle. "Yep," he said, "I guess you have at that— if the story reads the way you're telling it. If A.T. is using the *Phoenix* to get you out of their hair, and you're on to it, then if I tell 'em you're on to it. . . ."

Stan grinned back at the square-set yard supervisor. "Now let's try rumor number two," he said quietly. "The one that says I'm happy with A.T. That one's true, too. I'm happier than hell with A.T. I'm not very happy with how it's being run, or where it's going under present management—but A. T. isn't going that way much longer, nor will it be run by those boobs much longer."

Tobey slid down into his desk chair and leaned back happily. "Hell," he said, "I could get killed in an accident just for listening to you. I hear you, good, Star. What's the plan?"

"Well." Stan picked up pencil and pad. "Obviously, the *Phoenix* has got to have her own power system, independent of the K-class. And obviously it will have to be installed without A.T. knowing she's got it."

Tobey raised one eyebrow. "She's a one-hundred-twelve-gigaton mass, Star. If you've got a drive for her, you've got what they *know* to be impossible. You could install it in front of their noses and they wouldn't believe it. Don't know as I would either," he added.

"Then take a look and see what you think." Stan began sketching rapidly. "While you're refitting the *Phoenix*, could you whomp up a Tesla coil system like this"—he continued to sketch—"that reacts with the first nuclear resonance level of a lithium hydrogen reaction?" Swiftly he drew lines on a skeletalized outline of the *Phoenix*.

"We could feed hydrogen in here . . . and lithium right through . . . here. The plasma reaction center will be contained by an alternating field effect. And we sweep the reaction products out by supplying the hydrogen under pressure. We should wind up with a tight little fusion reactor which would put out plenty of power, I'd think. Plenty. Even for a gigaton mass like the *Phoenix*."

Tobey was staring at the sketch. "I'll . . . be . . . damned," he said slowly. "Well, I'll be damned." He looked up at Stan with respect. "Now why couldn't I have thought of that one? A Tesla drive." Then his face clouded. "But look—a drive like that will sure push the *Phoenix* around the system. It sure will be lethal to anything that gets in its wash. And the yards—they'll be the first things in that wash."

Stan nodded. "That's why we've got to get those K-class aboard. We've got to hold this—well, you're right; it's a Tesla drive—until we've got distance. Use the K's to boost us away from the Belt."

"But look, Star. With that drive, you ought to be able to pick up your own fuel on the way, if you had a magnetic pickup system. There's plenty of fuel in the solar wind to be picked up with a proper focusing mechanism. You could use this drive as a matchstick, say, to light a little hydrogen-fusion candle at some distance behind your tail, which would be held in place by the focusing coils that collected the protons. It would make a real good ramjet."

Stan frowned. Then his face cleared and brightened. "By damn, you're right. And you could make a magnetic lens . . . hmmm . . . set up external field coils like this. . . ." He sketched rapidly, pulled more paper to him, sketched some more, Tobey following his outline and sketching in details of his own.

Finally; *"That,"* Stan said, "should set us up a magnetic effect that would trap all the hydrogen drive could use, and funnel it into a nice little hydrogen reaction sun at about twenty-five kilometers off the stern. Right?"

Tobey went over the sketch again, drawing out the fields with his finger, seeming awed even at the touch of the sketch. Then; "It works," he said. "With that nickel-iron for a core, I expect we can get plenty of magnetic field for that system. Why, you could drive anything with that. Not just the *Phoenix.* You could—you could drive a small planet with that, and keep its sun right handy behind it. . . ."

Stan leaned back, staring at Tobey. "A planet," he said softly. "A small planet. With its own sun. Tobey, that's the answer to the quasars. Some people said they might be planets with their own drives, going space-hopping. And they were right. Tobey, we're going to the stars. Not just the system, the *stars!*"

"With the *Phoenix?*" Tobey seemed nonplused.

"Hell, no, not with the *Phoenix*. There's one little point in the Einstein equations that makes it pretty damned important to take a good-sized shipload when you go, you know; and to take along conditions under which a man can live a fairly normal life. With a drive designed like this, we could get to Galaxy Center in twenty-one years. Take a year to build up to light speeds, then we cross the galaxy in no time. But that's nothing, shipboard time. If you go out one hundred thousand light-years in a ship and then come back . . . well, there's two hundred thousand years of history has happened between you and the time you left. It's fun to think about. But without enough people along that speak your language, and without a home base that you can tolerate to stay on, it might get pretty damned upsetting.

"No, Tobey. This makes it possible, and we're going to the stars. But not on the *Phoenix*. We were going to set up Io as a colony—shucks, we'll set her up as a good-sized galactic scoutship. With what you might call a Tesla Tesseract drive. Call it a Teslaract drive for short. . . ."

Tobey considered this quietly for a long time. Then his face creased back into a huge grin. "A

Teslaract drive—and a planet for a ship. Yep. I buy that."

Then he leaned forward. "Now," he said brusquely, "I reckon that takes care of the long-range planning. But before we get to Jupiter to get to Io to build our scoutship, we need the *Phoenix*. And we need to get her ready before A.T. gets wise or changes its mind. So we can . . ."

It was several hours before the two of them drew back from pages of sketches, satisfied that the preliminary work for the immediate project was well underway.

Leaning back in his chair, Tobey nodded to himself, watched the satisfied expression on Stan's face. "I'll start getting that crew together tonight," he said.

"Picked crew, Tobey. All of them information-tight. But just in case there's a spy. . . ."

"There won't be any spies, Star."

Stan looked at Tobey, realized that he meant it, and nodded. "Okay. But take my word for one thing: no gold belts. Not on your crew. Don't trust a gold belt unless I give you the word to trust him. Okay?"

"I know about gold belts, Star. What I don't know is why you're wearing a gold belt."

Stan looked down at it ruefully. "Yeah," he said. "I'm wearing one. And it's going to be a thing to wear proudly one of these days. I think I've got some answers. But until I'm sure I'm right, don't trust a gold belt. I guess that's got to include me, too, doesn't it?"

They both laughed, but Stan thought there was still a hollow sound behind that laugh.

8

In order to be rationally useful, information must have both a value and a relation. The biochemical body has a system of logic circuits in its functions of maintenance, action and repair; and a near-infinite filing system in its DNA/RNA function of exact, or digital value, information storage, and retrieval. This filing is loosely analogous to a punched-card system. A virus acts effectively as a punched card. This system will react to any information filed on an exact-value basis. Relationality, or the analog function, is that of the field-storage system, which works on the basis of holographic recording.

——Findings in Centric Analysis
#111564/77

Time. Time was the factor both at the Ace Yards and in the rim area at Belt City, where Lang and Stan were putting forty of A.T.'s top gold-belters through a system of study that was more strenuous than any of them had ever thought he could attempt.

Weed had almost caviled when Stan brought him the list of the gold-belters he wanted prioritied to his project; had spent long hours using the strongest command techniques he could dream up; but Stan had been adamant, and the theory of the "stronger loyalty of the trust I hold" overrrode Weed's objections.

"He's getting his money's worth in loyalty from the Belters," Stan told Lang grimly. "The propaganda's working. But I don't think he's planning to let the gold belts I've picked actually take off with the *Phoenix*. Not without a fight.

"I guess his moves in that direction will give us the timing of whatever move he plans against us."

Retraining the gold-belters was a touchy question in itself. That they were being questioned in their off-hours by Weed and his gang, Stan was sure. Therefore they could not be allowed to know what was being done, nor why; nor could the hypnotic commands themselves be touched, for these would be specifically tested. These could not be touched until after they were aboard the *Phoenix*. Not even in Paulsen.

What they could do was reclaim the straight educational information the students had been fed and put it under the students' own control. So the schooling this time was thorough, but the opposite of what they'd had before. The gold-belters were put through a system of personalized study as intense as it could be made; and the testing that ended each day demanded of each facts from the areas in which he'd been studying that day, brought out in questions which were designed to draw on background facts that had been molecularly transplanted into their memories during the old schooling. Over and over Lang insisted, "Give us as much background information as possible with your answers."

Only in Sandra could the hypnotic commands be pulled and canceled, but the work with Sandra was sufficient to make Stan and Lang feel sure they had the technique by which it could be done for all the students as soon as it was safe to do so.

Between trying to resolve the technical details at the school and the technical details at the yard, Stan felt as though he were putting himself through a course of study more intense than he'd ever attempted in his own education.

"I'm putting heavy magnetic coils in each of the K-class nests," Tobey told him at one point. "Coils capable of putting out a one hundred thousand gauss field."

"If you hit them with a field that heavy, you'll blow out every circuit in every K that's docked," Stan had objected.

"Not if we turn off their circuits first. And when we go under drive, I don't want to lose our K's out the back. A normal magnalock system just isn't designed to hold against real thrust."

Once he carefully invited one of the gold-belters whom he knew to be questioned by Weed to go with him to the *Phoenix*. "I've got to go over her stem to stern," he told the man. "Want to go along?"

The idea had worried Tobey, but it worked out as Stan had hoped. "He's got the preconceived notion that we're K-class powered. He won't be looking for a drive. He won't see it."

As it worked out, the man obviously looked at the obvious, unobtrusively looked for the unobvious, and asked questions that were intelligent enough, but that didn't touch on sensitive areas and this could be answered quite truthfully. By the time

they reached the nose, Stan quit worrying and
could put his own attention on the actual inspection
for himself.

They climbed past the huge nose plug into the
one-hundred-meter-diameter central nose tank,
and Stan pointed out the radiatorlike grid of tiny
tubes leading through the kilometer-thick heat-sink
walls of the scoop to secondary tanks that would
receive the liquefied gases from this initial compression compartment.

The Goldie shook his head. "The plasma wave in
front of this ship when it's diving into atmosphere at
a hundred kilometers a second should reach well
over a million degrees," he said thoughtfully. "I
don't see how you can cool that plasma sufficiently
to store it in any kind of container. It seems to me
she might melt."

Tobey looked at the man carefully. "Nope," he
said. "She won't melt. Primary cooling occurs by
radiation from the shock wave itself. Secondary
cooling, which is what you're referring to, will be by
ablation of the interior tank surfaces."

"But—"

"But that might melt the tanks down?" Stan interrupted, smiling. "You're darned right it will. But
you see, the material that melts will have no place
to go. The tank surfaces will be melted—actually,
evaporated—so that the gaseous metal will mix
with the plasma. But that will only be temporary.
The mass of the ship will be more than sufficient to
heat-sink all the energy involved. And as things cool
off, the metal will plate right back out of the plasma
onto the tank surfaces again. The metal that plates
back out will be contaminated and of low structural
strength, but the mass of the metal beyond it that
was not contaminated will have more than suffi-

cient strength for the pressures involved; and we expect that the spongy inner deposit will be used over and over again, as a sort of ablative lining."

"But what about the outer surface?"

"The outer surface will ablate to some extent while we're filling the scoop. Then we close the plugs and repel a good part of the plasma ahead of the ship with a vibrating magnetic field. Plasma is a highly conductive medium. It will be repelled by the field and will not touch the nose of the ship. This will reduce the ablation, although we'll still get a tremendous amount of heat. But she'll take it. She's a *big* heat sink."

Tobey chuckled. "That ablative plasma is a real problem, though, Stan. You should have been here while we were trying to mill those tubes through. Every time we turned on the cutting beam, it would plate out all over us—helmets, hoses, laser, the works. You'd get a split-second cut and a three hour clean-up job before you could operate again. We finally put a T-clamp over each place we were going to mill, with a window that we could fire the laser through and a sort of vacuum cleaner pipe to take out the vaporized metal from the T. That way all we had to do was feed a moving belt of film plastic across the window so that we had a constantly clear surface through which to work."

"Did you have the same problem in all your milling operations?" the Goldie asked.

"Yeah. We solved the one on the outside, and we still use the same solution in all exterior milling operations. It's a matter of electric charge. If the body you're milling is highly charged to a negative potential, you can set up screens of the opposite charge, and the vapor plates right out on them. Otherwise we'd have had contaminating vapor drifting all over the yards, plating out on everything it touched. Of course, chunks that come off are no problem. If they're big enough to catch, we catch 'em. If they're not big enough to catch, we just let 'em go."

Time. The three months originally predicted passed, and the work went on. Two more months passed, and although everybody was at stretch, both jobs nearing completion, the work was not done. Then in the middle of the sixth month, Stan got Tobey on a tight beam channel.

"Tobey," he said, choosing his words with care, "it's gotta be go. Now. Say, three days."

Tobey chewed his lip. "Yeah," he said. "I'm getting the signals, too. Okay, it's go. Three days. Make it seventy-two hours from now."

"Right. And Tobey. Clear your crew from the B for baby crew area as of now. And seal it off from the A and C areas, but leave the corridors from the locks and officers' country open."

Tobey raised one eyebrow quizzically, but all he said was "Right," and without another word Stan signed off. Then he called Paulsen up to the monitor's desk from which he was supervising the work going on in forty cubicles.

"Is the *Sassy Lassie* fueled?" he asked, knowing that it was.

"Sure, boss," said Paulsen.

"Fine. So is my *Erika Three*. I'm canceling classes. Can you lift twenty-two men out to Ace Yards?"

"When? Now? Give me a couple of hours to get food aboard and duffel . . ."

"No food. No duffel. Right now. The *Phoenix* is just twelve hours from here."

"Fourteen with a load like that."

"Fourteen hours from here. Our gold belts have

never seen her. Thought we'd just jaunt over and take a look. You take Dr. Lang and half the class. I'll take Sandra and the other half."

"Just jaunt over, take a look, and jaunt back? Thought you'd wait until we were ready to move aboard, then spend a couple of weeks aboard familiarizing."

"Yeah." Stan leaned back in the monitor's seat, relaxed and smiling. "That's what I plan. But a look-see in the meantime . . . I don't know. I figure they're getting a little stale and a little impatient. A jaunt out there would break the monotony. Where you tied up?"

"Tube one-eleven."

"Okay. Don't even tell them where we're going. Let it be a surprise. Call them all in here, cancel all classes. I'll order up enough strutcars, and we'll take off."

Stan, with his half of the class, reached the *Phoenix* first, sent Sandra to the bridge, the gold-belters along to Common Room B that centered one of the three independent crew areas, each complete with galley, freshers, and cabins; each connected by corridor to each of the other two crew areas; a corridor to the locks aft of the ship; and a corridor forward to officers' country, itself a self-contained area with its own common room, galley, freshers, and more commodious cabins. Forward of officers' country was the bridge, and beside the bridge his own office and personal quarters. Beyond the bridge was the four kilometers of virgin nickel iron that would take up heat from the scoop tank set in the nose.

Having seen that his part of the class was safely in the common room, Stan stationed himself by the nest assigned to the *Sassy Lassie*. As soon as that ship had magnalocked in, he made his way through the air locks.

"Turn off all circuits—now," he told Paulsen.

Paulsen started to obey reflexively. Then his hand hesitated on the switch. "Hadn't I better leave her on standby?" he asked.

"Not this time," said Stan authoritatively, and before Paulsen could object further, he'd pulled himself back out of the air lock into the corridor.

When Katsu Lang and Paulsen, with the first of the gold-belters immediately behind them, pulled through into the corridor, Stan was waiting.

"Dr. Lang," he said, "you go on through to the bridge. Sandra's waiting for you there. Paulsen, you and your men gather in Common Room B. It's right down that corridor," he said, pointing.

Then he waited again until the last of the gold-belters was into the corridor before turning and closing the bulkhead behind them, activating bolts that would seal it off until someone released them from the bridge.

Following the men to the common room assigned them, he quickly counted to be sure they were all there, then climbed on a table, gesturing for them to gather around him.

"We are leaving almost immediately," he told them firmly. There was an instant clamor, which he silenced with a raised hand. "We will have two weeks aboard to become familiar with how this ship works. By the time we reach Jupiter orbit, we will either know that we have around us a good, sound ship and a good working crew, or that we should turn back. I have no intention of turning back," he added. "If we win, we will be opening a colony about the size of Earth's moon, and our next step will be the stars. If we lose—well, that won't mean much to anybody but us.

"I brought you aboard by surprise," he said into a quiet that was the first reaction to shock. "We have enemies. Those enemies will try to stop us. You are aboard and will stay aboard. I will talk to you again before we go under thrust."

With that he jumped down from the table and made his way to the bulkhead toward officers' country. He had crossed the bulkhead and secured it behind him before anyone had recovered sufficiently to try to stop him.

Now they were locked in. The best brains of A.T. kidnapped right out from under Weed's nose and secured in a nickel-iron prison in space.

Stan reached the bridge to find Tobey and two of his crew waiting with Sandra and Katsu Lang.

"Have you got two men who can handle a K-class?" Stan asked Tobey without preliminary.

"Any one of us can, Star," Tobey answered.

"Okay. Put a man on the *Erika* and one on the *Sassy Lassie*. We've got to use them to swing the *Phoenix* so she's at right angles to the yard. We may have to take off on our own drive power, and I don't want to crisp the docks."

Tobey looked at him quizzically. "I just got word that our fourteen K-class are on their way," he said. "I gather they lifted from Belt City about six hours after you did. ETA about eight hours."

"In that case, let's get the *Phoenix* swung just as fast as we can. It may take a few hours to position her right, and I want her swung and the men inboard before those K's arrive."

"You really think Weed will make a move to take over the ship instead of letting us take off?" Lang asked.

Stan looked at the Mentor in surprise. "Of course. He's got to. He's not planning to lose his forty top goldies! He'd do it even to keep from losing Tobey's crew, but it hasn't occurred to him yet that they're vulnerable.

"No," Stan went on, "he's got to make his move now. We took him by surprise, loading the belters aboard, and he's off balance. But he'll move. I expect those fourteen K's are loaded to the gills with soldiers, and we'll be in the middle of a first-class war in about eight hours.

"But meantime, Dr. Lang, you and Sandra can start setting up Common Room A for the dehypnosis techniques. You can't start the actual work until after the war, but, assuming we win, I can free up a few men then to help you. You can get the place ready now, and you'll have two weeks on the way to Jupiter to do the job."

When the fourteen K-class ships showed, flying a tight pattern, it was Tobey who talked them into the nests, assigning each one its berth and berthing time, yakking informally but with authority to the pilots, screening each one of them as he gave them instructions, and getting each one into a pattern of communication as he worked.

As the third ship magnalocked in, he switched his screen off and spoke to Stan, who was carefully out of range of the video.

"The pilots are alone in the control cabins," he said, "but I rather think you're right that there are other men aboard. Probably fifteen to twenty per ship."

Stan grinned crookedly. "It's a fair bet there are," he said.

"And, Star . . . these men are Earthies. There's

not a Belter pilot aboard."

"Oh?" Stan paused. "You sure?"

"Hell no, I'm not sure," Tobey said. "But I'd lay odds on it."

Stan nodded, then said, "If you can spot the command ship, bring it in last."

. "I think I've got it spotted, and it even seems to be maneuvering to be last in. Okay."

Tobey switched the screen back on and the process of talking the ships in continued. As the last ship was berthed, there was a long pause. Then Tobey's screen lighted to show the pilot of the final ship.

"Control officer," the man said grimly, "the locks aren't opening. What is the problem?"

Tobey raised his head to the screen as though from concentrated effort. "I don't know," he said. "I was just trying to find out. I seem to be having some trouble with the magnalock system."

"Well, get it fixed and let us out," the voice said sternly. Tobey kept the screen on while he busied himself over the control console, biting on his lips in vexation. Then he turned again to the screen.

"Have your pilots shut down all circuits for a minute," he said. "I'm going to send a power surge through the magnalock system to see if I can free it, but it might be enough to blow a weak circuit in a ship, and it'd be better if they were off."

"Who are you?" the man on the screen demanded fiercely.

Tobey looked at him in surprise. "Tobey Olsen," he said finally. "Supervisor of the Ace yards. Who are you?"

"Is Dustin aboard?" the man asked.

Tobey raised one eyebrow as though considering whether to object to the brusque treatment, then shrugged his shoulders. "I believe Mr. Dustin is

with his crew and scientific personnel. They are"—
his voice held light sarcasm—"familiarizing themselves with the ship. If it will make you happier, I
can have him called to the bridge."

"No. No, leave him to his toys. Very well. I'll
have my men come off standby for a minute."

"Fine," said Tobey. "I'll give it a shot. If that
doesn't work, I'll have to send a man down to open
the locks manually."

There was a pause while the pilot on the screen
spoke into an intercom system. Then; "Very well,
Olsen. All ships except this one have shut down,
and I'm doing so now." There was a click, and the
screen went blank.

Instantly Tobey threw the switch that would
send a surge of one hundred thousand gauss
through each of the magnalocks to which the ships
were joined—enough locking energy to hold the
ships against a ten-G thrust; and enough stray
magnetism to prevent the operation of any radio or
electric motor on board. The fourteen K's were
locked on, silenced, frozen in place. Helpless.

Then Tobey turned to Stan. "Your birds are secure, Star," he said. "Sure you don't want to just
leave them aboard their ships? For a little, anyhow,
until they learn who's boss?"

"No," said Stan. "Best we continue the operating
procedure and get them the hell out of the way."
Taking his seat at his own console, he activated a
screen in the corridor outside the locks. Tobey's
twenty men were standing there, fully armed and at
the ready.

Tobey had already activated his own screen and
was speaking to his men. "Looks like what we've
got aboard those ships is about twenty Earthie soldiers per," he said. "Think you can handle 'em?"

He was greeted with a roar of pleasure.

"Okay," he said. "Start with Lock Two. And boys," he added, "leave lock one-forty-four until last. That one's got the command personnel aboard."

Stan watched, forcing back the tension that threatened to keep him from a clear head, as Tobey's crew began hand-manipulating the inner lock. This one they opened all the way; then five of them disappeared within. The outer lock would be opened only far enough for one man to squeeze through, according to plan, and . . .

He could hear shouts and mumblings. A long time passed, but finally one man stumbled out of the lock into the arms of the waiting crew, followed a minute later by a small arsenal of personal weapons. The man was frisked again in the corridors, then shoved toward C section by one of Tobey's men, who held a gun to his back. Watching the man closely, Stan realized that Tobey had been right: these men were Earthies. He wasn't sure just what small clues gave the man away, but the Earthie background showed plainly.

Another followed, and another. It was a slow process.

When fifteen had come through, one of the crewmen came out and called toward the screen: "They say that's all of them."

"Don't believe it," Tobey answered. "Tell the rest they've got just three minutes to come out, then we're going to sleep-gas their ship and seal it. They'll be there for at least two weeks, if they want to spend that long in suits."

There was a pause, and Tobey began timing it. At the end of the three minutes he called again: "Come on out, boys. Then sleep-gas that one and seal it."

Emptying the second ship was a similar task, but it seemed to go faster. Tobey's crew was getting familiar with the operation. There were sixteen out this time before word came that that was all.

This time Tobey changed his command. "Take the last man out of that ship, send him into the other to see that we meant what we said. Then send him back for any more men that may be in his ship."

The last man out, disarmed and disheveled from a thorough search for small arms, was brought up, given a low pressure suit and a diox shot, and the lock on the first was unsealed. Five crewmen disappeared into the lock with him. Several minutes passed, then the Earthie came running from the lock, holding his arm, followed shortly by the five crewmen. One addressed the screen while the others sealed the lock.

"They thought he was one of us," Tobey was told succinctly. "They shot at him."

"Good." Tobey's voice was grim. "Now send that man back into his own ship, and let him tell them the story."

Shortly, from the second lock, men began appearing again, until the ship had disgorged twenty. When word came that that was all, Tobey instructed his men to use the wounded man as a shield, and go in to search the ship. It was all clear.

It took hours, but the crews came out. Until they reached the final ship.

"Before you tackle that one," Tobey instructed, lines of strain showing around his grim mouth, "have one of the men from the first crew write a note. Get it shoved through the lock to the men in the first ship. See if they want to take advantage of a final offer, or if they prefer to stay where they are at our convenience, which will be a long time coming."

This time the remaining five men capitulated, and the only ship still unsealed was the one that nested in 144.

"Now," said Tobey, "bring out the wounded man from that second ship. He's had first aid? Good. Send him through, alone, into the command ship, and have him explain the situation. If they want to capitulate, they can come out the way the others have—one at a time. If not, they stay where they are, and we sleep-gas the ship."

The man went in and the minutes passed. It seemed to Stan that time stood still. The inner lock on the 144 stood open; five of Tobey's crew were inside the lock. The outer lock was, presumably, open enough to admit one man.

Finally, the wounded man came out, was searched and sent on to Area C. Stan found himself holding his breath—until a second man came out, and the former process was on again.

The twentieth man out this time was in full Earth uniform, and Stan caught his breath as the men of Tobey's crew turned him this way and that, searching him as thoroughly as the others, but, Stan noted, with a care that showed a deference for his insignia.

It was the general, Stan realized. The general that he had met once before, in Professor Mallard's office in the school at Prudhoe Bay on Earth.

"Bring the general to the bridge," he heard himself saying, while his mind raced back and forth across—was it only a year?—that separated him from that moment in time; from that boy who had not known whether to believe he was a robot; but who had known very surely that he would not—that he *could* not—be a robot for the military.

9

The eidetic-response nature of the information-filing systems makes a glut of unanalyzed information in the systems a major hazard. Such filings can be devastating when they are retrieved and put to use without having had serious conscious (interface) attention on their recall and review. With a sufficient input of unevaluated information, the individual becomes irrational, acting out on a stimulus/response basis the unanalyzed, literal logic handed up to him by his information-storage systems.

——Findings in Centric Analysis
#111664/77

The general was seated on the far side of the desk from Stan. Tobey's man, Jarl, was lounging in the doorway with a stun gun, where he could keep an eye on him. Tobey himself was seated against the wall.

If the general noticed the guard, he gave no indication; he merely began to raise the hand that held a signet ring, to place it on the desk where Stan could see it. That gesture, Stan noted, was made in such a way that the ring was hidden from Jarl. It couldn't be hidden from Tobey, and the general didn't try to disguise his action in that direction, but let his eyes go to the signet ring. Stan let his own eyes follow them.

Then, in a voice of authority, the general spoke: "I, the trainer, speak. You obey."

From the corner of his eye Stan saw Tobey jerk forward and Jarl drew himself up, but he gestured to them both.

"Never mind," he said. "It doesn't work on me." Then, to the general: "Remember? I'm the robot who refused to robe."

The general smiled, twisting the ring on his finger. "It always did seem a little too pat to me, Dustin. Very well. For the present, at least, it seems to be your move." He looked up, the smile gently twisting his lips.

Stan found himself admiring the man. A professional to his fingertips. "What do you mean, 'for the present, at least'?" he asked.

The general relaxed into his seat, but the motion in no way decreased the basic military exactness of his bearing. "I could, of course," he said genially, "stand on my right to give my name, rank and serial number and to refuse other information. But that seems hardly justified in"—he stared slowly around him, at Tobey, at the small cabin—"congenial circumstances. Instead I should prefer simply to tell you that I am authorized to give you clearance to Jupiter to continue your mission."

Stan nodded to himself. "That's why you brought two hundred and ninety four men to board me—fully armed?" he asked.

"Oh, we didn't plan to let you take the gold-belters along. But I think we might have spared you fourteen pilots to K-boost you to orbit. Then you and Dr. Lang and the young lady could have remained aboard. Paulsen was to be allowed to remain as well."

"Thanks," said Stan. "Kind of you, I suppose."

"You'd have had the *Sassy Lassie*. You could possibly have made something of the trip."

Stan laughed. The general looked at him thoughtfully.

"I think, however, that under present circumstances . . ." He allowed his voice to drop, then continued. "Since things have taken a different turn from that which we, ah, expected, I have sufficient authority to allow you to proceed with your gold-belters, and to keep the K's, once you have put my men"—he paused, and sketched a glance at Tobey, over his shoulder at the guard—"and Olsen's, down at the docks."

Stan smiled gently. "General," he said, "I must admit that you have gained my sincere admiration. It takes real guts, sir, to sit here in my office, my prisoner, and try to make terms that will set you safely back in the Belt. Earthies in the Belt," he said softly. "Earthie soldiers in the Belt. You took off from Belt City," he added.

The general looked at him speculatively. "A small garrison," he said nonchalantly. "Available. So we used them."

"We?"

The general shrugged. Stan's face grew hard. "Weed," he said at last. "He took over at A.T. so easily—almost as if it were a setup, with powerful backing. I should have guessed. A tool of Earth?''

The general's face remained bland, and Stan went on. "And he is the one who has been beating the drums for war with Earth—a war that the Belt was scheduled to lose? A Fleet war that would be backed up by a fifth column in the Belt."

He waited, but the general remained silent.

"A small garrison, you say. That becomes doubtful. But how many could you have hidden in the Belt? Perhaps a few hundred more in Belt City, if you kept them in quarters. Then you'd have been depending on a certain number of gold-belters in key points of control . . . hmm. I *did* upset your plans by kidnapping this particular forty, didn't I?"

He stared at the general, who had fixed his attention on the ceiling, but couldn't hide the dark red color that began to suffuse his neck and face.

"Well," said Stan. "Well." Then he leaned forward and keyed the intercom to the bridge. When the screen lighted, he saw Tobey's man, Barnes, at the control console.

"Mr. Barnes," he said, "get the Belt News Service on the wire and ask where Earth Fleet is currently maneuvering." Then he leaned back and waited. The general's face had gone from red to white and was now coloring again.

It was several minutes before the word came through. "Last reports, sir, believed correct to about twenty-four hours ago: Earth in Gemini sector, and the fleet is reported maneuvering Beltwards of Earth."

"And—let's see. Belt City is in Capricorn. Jupiter is . . . just entering Sagittarius. Thank you, Mr. Barnes."

Stan switched off and turned to Tobey. "That

puts Earth Fleet a bit over two weeks from Belt City at top acceleration. We should have at least that long before Weed is convinced that the general and his forces are irretrievably gone. He'll think that the general is using the K's to boost us to a Hohmann orbit as planned before coming back. It won't occur to him that we coud knock out a force of two hundred ninety-four Earth soldiers, especially when he thinks our goldies are under hypnotic control to the general, and that you're just aboard, Tobey.

"So I'd think we have at least two weeks before Weed can be convinced and can convince Earth that their schedule is shot to pieces, their cover is blown, and that they'd better scrap their timetable and attack on a crash priority basis; plus two weeks to get to the Belt. That gives us, say, twenty-eight days, plus or minus a few, to go to Jupiter and get back to intercept Earth Fleet."

"But—"

"Could take them longer than that, since they don't know we've got any kind of drive but the K-class. It will take us about twelve days to reach Jupiter, and another twelve to get back between Earth Fleet and Belt City. If we don't scare 'em, I would guess we've got plenty of time for at least one dive through Jupiter's atmosphere, and that will load our tanks for some . . . tricks."

Grinning to himself, Stan turned to the general. "I think," he said, "that you have given us insufficient credit. Your timetable does not seem to have been keyed to the departure of the *Phoenix*."

The general's voice sounded only slightly choked as he answered, "I do not understand your reference to a timetable, Dustin. And just what interest do you think the takeoff of the *Phoenix* for a ramscoop project on Jupiter could have to Earth Fleet?"

"Every interest, if they were right bright," Stan said coldly.

Suddenly the general's voice rose to a bellow: "Surely you don't think this"—his voice choked off and his arm waved around to indicate the ship— "this *ramscoop* hunk could take on Earth Fleet? What do you think you are, a one-ship Goliath protecting the entire Belt orbit with a nickel-iron canister that doesn't even mount a cannon?"

As abruptly as he had lost his control, the general regained it. He leaned back, chortling almost normally. "A cannonless canister," he repeated, eyes glinting shrewdly at Stan. "Son," he said, his voice taking on a kindly patriarchal tone, "you'd better take my offer while the taking's good."

Instead of answering, Stan turned to the guard in the doorway. "Jarl," he said, "quarter the general in one of the officer's suites under constant guard; one outside the suite, one inside with him. Take even the door to the fresher down. He is not to be by himself for one minute. It'll tie up some men," he added, "but I think it's a good idea."

As the guard left with the general, Stan turned to the chunky figure in the chair by the wall. "Tobey," he said, "we'll need sixteen pilots to boost us off with the K's, but once we're boosted, those sixteen will be free for guard work. We only need a crew of two on the bridge, besides yourself and me. We'll take watch about, so that's four men besides ourselves. We'll need four men to work with Dr. Lang and Sandra, in case they have any trouble with the gold-belters while they're running the de-hypnosis techniques, but that can wait until after

we've boosted. And we'll need guards on the C
area, using both videoscreen for monitoring and
normal bulkhead guard. It looks like every one of
your men will be on heavy duty for a good long bit
now. Think they can handle it?"

Tobey nodded, grinning. "It's a picked crew,
Star. They can handle."

"All right, then. We get under way as fast as you
can assign your men to their jobs. The *Phoenix* is a
ramscoop . . . uh, canister," he added grimly, "and
it's time she started cannoning."

The banded face of Jupiter was glaring in the
control cabin screen, its fluorescence like a vari-
colored neon sign, with not one bit of surface detail
visible from whatever might lie below the neon glow
of the upper atmosphere.

"Weigh ship, Mr. Barnes." Stan spoke quietly,
and the mate went through a series of switch-flip-
ping operations as he said, "Aye, sir."

There was a brief surge of fluctuation in the drive
gravs, and Barnes spoke without taking his eyes off
the panel. "Gross mass, 112,535,970,543,196
tonnes, sir."

"Very good, Mr. Barnes. Enter in the log and
sound action stations."

The hoot that sounded action stations went out
over the intercom, dulled to a distant murmur in
the control cabin.

"Main drives off. Relative velocity to be
monitored continuously. Inertial guidance . . ."

The ship was now on its own. Without drive, it
was falling like a rock toward the huge planet
below, aimed nearly directly for the equatorial belt
and just toward the edge of the disk in a plotted

flight that would take it around the curve to the
east. Yet the comparison was more accurately that
of a bullet, fired at maximum thrust and aimed on
target; perhaps the swiftest bullet that man had
ever fired. The five kilometer chunk of nickel-iron
that was the *Phoenix* would penetrate the atmosphere with a velocity of more than one hundred
kilometers per second; and would skip out the other
side like a bullet striking through a wax target.

Yet everyone aboard was conscious of the fact
that at that velocity wax, or water, or even the pre-
dominantly hydrogen gas that is Jupiter's atmosphere, will put up massive resistance. The
whole attention of everyone on the bridge was riveted to the droning voice that kept repeating rate of
approach and time; and in an instinctive gesture for
those confined to the cabins and crew areas aft,
Stan reached forward and keyed the voice into the
ship's intercom.

The figure for relative velocity was increasing,
slowly but inexorably, under the tug of gravity from
the giant beneath them; the distance and time de-
creasing; and then . . .

"... ten seconds, 106.23. Nine seconds ..." The
kilometers per second implied by the second figure
was understood. There wasn't time to give more
than the number itself.

The first tenuous clutches of decelerating G force
from the fringes of the heavy atmosphere began to
give them a new sense of gravitic orientation. The
control room swung on its gimbals and the G-force
oriented to the floor. At first it was only a feather
touch, and the faintest of whistles; but already the
ship was surrounded by a fiery air of plasma that
obscured all vision and would blank out any at-

tempt at communication.

The seconds were ticking off; and now there was a new reading added to the list, although it wasn't read out. The rate of ablation of the thick steel shell that formed the bullet-head of the bullet was being ticked off in millimeters and then in centimeters; and the craft was gradually slowed in the thick friction of the atmosphere.

The G-needle climbed and climbed, and the droning voice that had been counting the seconds and the relative velocity was now reading G's and velocity. "Point nine G, 106.21; point nine one G,. . ."

"Boy, I'll bet the contrail we're leaving can be seen all the way back to the Belt," the navigator commented suddenly into the tension that overlay the voice of the count.

Without moving his attention a hair's breadth from the control panel before him, Stan ordered: "Gigged for none-essential communication, Mr. Roth."

"Tank pressure 250,000 p.s.i., sir," came from another console.

"Close the valves and activate the repulsion field, Mr. Morely."

"Aye, sir."

In the nose of the ship, four and a half kilometers away, the huge tank plug was snapped into place by a magnetic field; and at the same time a pulsating magnetic field was generated over the whole nose of the ship, repelling the conductive plasma wave away from the bow so that ablation might be reduced. The plug, white-hot from the stream of gases that had passed it, would weld firmly into its tapered seat, but that didn't matter since a new plug would have to be milled before the operation could be repeated.

"Valves closed, sir. Pressure declining."

As the heat sink around the main tank absorbed heat from the gases, the pressure would decline near zero; and the gases forced through the kilometer-long radiator surface of the first compression tank would be trickling out as liquids into the subsidiary tanks.

Then, almost as suddenly as it had come, the G-force dropped. The control room swung slowly on its gimbals to take up a new position oriented toward the planet they had passed. The lightest of tidal forces—less than one-tenth of a G—was still tugging them back; but they were clear of the atmosphere and back in space.

"Whew! That's ten minutes I'll—"

"Another gig, Mr. Roth. Mr. Barnes, warm up the drive."

"Aye, sir."

Another G-force appeared as the drive-tubes went into action and the control cabin swung once again on its gimbals, oriented now stern-down in the normal manner of drive acceleration.

"Weigh the ship, Mr. Barnes."

Again Barnes's fingers danced nimbly over the keyboard, and his voice came back, "129,191,294,183,589 tonnes, sir. Looks like we picked up just about sixteen point six six times ten to the twelfth tonnes, sir. But the estimated loss of mass was point one percent, which would mean that our actual pickup was"—the fingers danced again—"fourteen point seven percent of gross weight, sir."

Stan smiled grimly. "Thank you, Mr. Barnes,"

he said, then added almost to himself, "and now we have a tight ship with a proven crew and full tanks of compressed liquid gas. We can go hunting."

"Sir?"

"Mr. Roth. Before those vocal cords of yours make it imperative that I dismiss you from the bridge, plot a course for the *Phoenix* to cross just ahead of Belt City's orbital position, and to intersect a line from the sun approximately halfway between the Belt and Mars orbit."

"Yes, sir."

"And Mr. Roth. You might use those vocal cords —*sotto voce*, of course—to pray that I'm right in my guesstimate of just where and when we will find Earth Fleet."

10

The art of learning is seen to be not just the absorption of information and its filing for retrieval and use, but the periodic calling up and review of all pertinent information when new is added; and a search for information buried too deeply in the system to be easily retrieved during action periods. When the system of learning includes these factors, it achieves breathtaking dimension.

——Findings in Centric Analysis
#111764/77

It was a guess. It was purely a guess, and like a game of chess, the number of other moves that Earth Fleet might make formed an astronomical figure.

Yet, like chess, those moves were limited to the area of the board, so long as the goal was Belt City and a war to destroy the independence of the Belt.

And it had to be Belt City, for the Belt would be won or lost there. Belt City was where the Earth garrison of troops would be hidden.

Yet—the fleet could move on a variety of courses that would show a high exponential curve factor even in the probability area, and searching space by guesswork to locate the blinkers that would identify a fleet in motion was playing tag blindfolded in the dark, Stan knew. For there to be any hope of success, the search would have to be narrowed to a comparatively minute sector.

When he took the problem to Tobey, the answer was immediate.

"Hell," said Tobey, "me and the crew, we know almost every skipper in the Belt—and Belt ships are all over the place. I'll send out word we want to know where Earth Fleet is. We'll get it."

"But Tobey! The Fleet will be on radio silence and deep secret maneuvers."

"Won't make a nevermind," Tobey snorted. "There's no fleet made that can keep its whereabouts secret if you've got enough eyes watching from enough places."

But as the *Phoenix* sped on its swift flight sunward, across Capricorn toward Aquarius, the queries that sped ahead of it brought no satisfactory results. Rumors came back by the dozen; rumors that placed Earth Fleet all over the system. But no hard facts. Nothing on which to focus a camera.

The queries grew more insistent; the replies more vaguely irrational. "Earth Fleet reported maneuvering Beltward in Taurus. No evidence."

"Earth Fleet reported on a Mars course toward Libra. . ."

Yet as the reports came in the cameras went into action; each sector named was filmed. After the twentieth report, Stan gave up sitting personally and looking at the blinking pattern of the stars that portrayed what they should see against what the camera said was there, in back-and-forth switching arrangements that would make any anomalous object stand out as a blinking on-off pattern; while the fixed and unmoving objects that were the farther stars would remain shining steadily on the screen. They spotted blinkers time after time, but blinkers that were normal Belt debris—either asteroids or ships—but no fleet.

And the factors of velocity and vector that are the basic factors of space flight were drawing the deadline closer for any course change that would intersect—if the fleet were actually readying to attack Belt City.

Stan held himself calm on the bridge, but off duty he paced his office. Suppose Earth Fleet were refusing to react to the factors that *dictated* immediate action? he asked himself.

No. They had to react now, or sacrifice the buildup of their garrison in Belt City. They had to react before the *Phoenix* returned to alert the Belt to the entire plot. They *had* to react. And the only sensible reaction was immediate attack.

Then—an almost laconic message from a Belt prospector in Aquarius near the Capricorn line. "Bogies on my screen. Too far to be more than bogies. Could be a whish of asteroids out of orbit. But could be your fleet." The message was addressed to Tobey who brought it instantly to Stan.

"Reckon that's them, Star?"

Stan stared at the message. "Who's your man, Tobey?"

"Prospector. A good one. He doesn't spook easy. When he says bogies, there are bogies. When he says they could be our fleet, he means there are enough of them and the characteristics are there. But he has no info on why they should be there; and they could be something else, so he's not about to commit himself."

"You think it's them?"

Tobey grinned. "I know damned well," he said. "When Jim added it could be a whish of asteroids out of orbit, he knows asteroids don't go out of orbit, and he was saying that those bogies weren't on Belt orbit. He was saying it was more likely Earth Fleet than anything else he could think of, but so far as he knows, there's no good reason for Earth Fleet to be there, so he's hedging."

Hope surged through Stan as he and Tobey set up the computer for a view of the prospector's sector. As Tobey manipulated the computer, Stan manipulated the camera, swung it onto the target area and matched the stars on the video screen as projected by the camera against the stars on the video screen projected by the computer.

Blink, blink. For a few moments, they were all blinking. And then, with the fine controls of the camera adjusted, they phased in gradually until the stars the computer said should be there and the stars the camera said were there fused and burned steady and clear on the screen.

There were many blinkers left after the background steadied out, and then those began to disappear as the computer picked off and identified the normal orbits of asteroids, leaving only the nonstandard orbits of ships.

Many of the ones that were left, Stan could disregard. They were obviously K-class, identifiable as much by their winking patterns as by their size. But there was one group left unidentified; and these he magnified up to the very limits of the ability of the electron screen to magnify the camera's image. The ghostly shapes were still mere pinpoints, but it was a group of at least twenty traveling in unison, and that, for Stan, was enough information.

"Okay, Tobey. Shift us on a zero-to-zero base leg ninety degrees from the orientation of that spot. Let's make our base two thousand kilometers. Triangulate the exact distance; then, after an hour, triangulate again. That'll give us their velocity."

For the next two hours, the *Phoenix* shifted back and forth across a line drawn from itself to the moving targets. The range was found, and the velocity; and it was very definite that its velocity would bring Earth Fleet to Belt City in fourteen days.

"We can just make it," Stan said, "with maybe two days to spare."

"Now hear this. Now hear this. All hands secure for high-G. Fifteen minutes."

Stan's eyes roved across the bridge as Paulsen's voice continued over the all-channel intercom, and his chin set slowly. He would have preferred to have Paulsen at the control officer's console. Barnes was competent—more than competent, as he'd proven. But Paulsen had a knack with a ship.

But not yet, he told himself. The hypnosis had been yanked; he was sure of it, and Lang had reassured him. Yet . . . not until there is absolute certainty, he told himself. Having him on the bridge at all, even at the communications console, was risk enough. He felt again the weight of the small hand stun-gun at his belt with which he had hedged when he had realized that he wanted Paulsen on the bridge almost as much as Paulsen wanted to be there.

The other gold-belters thought themselves free now of confinement; but he had given orders to Jarl that once they had secured for high-G, the bulkheads to their area were to be secured without their knowledge, and the action reported to him.

Yet who will trust the distrustful? he asked himself; and knew with a deep certainty that not only did the others trust him, he trusted himself; and that it was a hard-won trust.

"Area B secured, sir." It was Jarl's voice on his personal intercom.

"Thank you. Best you secure yourself for high-G now," he answered. Then to Paulsen; "Turn on screens and speakers throughout the ship so that every man, prisoner or crew, can watch and hear the action."

"Yes, sir," said Paulsen.

The minutes passed slowly. The *Phoenix* hung directly on the course of the oncoming Earth Fleet with an orbital velocity that matched her fairly well to the Belt, though she was inside it.

"Mr. Barnes. Are they closing satisfactorily?"

"Yes, sir. They were all bunched up, but now they're beginning to spread out as though they plan to pass us in a ring pattern. I think, sir, that they're trying to make us think they think we're a rock."

"Are they still decelerating?"

"No, sir. When they smoothed out into a ring, they began to let 'em drift. Closing velocity is now steady at seven point two four eight kilometers per second."

"And we're still nose-on to them?"

"Yes, sir." There was a note of light humor behind Barnes's voice. "Nose-on to the center of their ring, sir."

"Very well, Mr. Barnes. Operate the external proton beams to bring us up to ten KV negative charge." That would make the *Phoenix* negative in respect to Earth Fleet. Any metallic vapor discharged would be attracted to the Fleet.

Turning to the navigator's console where Tobey sat, relaxed, Stan saw him smiling, a grim smile with a fierceness tugging at the corners of his mouth, but a smile. Stan nodded quietly to himself and put his full attention on the screen before him.

"Laser range?" he asked.

"Five minutes to laser." Barnes's voice became taut as Earth Fleet seemed to leap toward them.

"Count down to their range of firing, Mr. Barnes."

"Estimated countdown, sir, is four minutes. Three. Two. One. In seconds; . . . thirty, twenty, ten, nine, eight, seven, six . . ."

The countdown passed zero and went to minus one, then minus two. . . .

There was a swirling glare that covered the forward viewscreens, but Barnes held the controls steady and Stan watched the second hand of the chronometer. Three seconds. Then a slight jar.

"Damage control, sir. They all bracketed the same center of the bow and penetrated number-one tank. We've lost approximately five hundred cubic meters of hull from that area, and tank pressure is falling over toward zero."

On the screen the cloud of roiling metallic vapor that had been five hundred cubic meters of solid nickel steel was drifting away from the *Phoenix*, racing ahead of them. Then, at first mistily and then more solidly, Earth Fleet appeared, pulling through the cloud of vapor, but scattering wildly as though they had attempted to miss its outer edges.

But there had been no misses. Each ship emerged from the cloud as shiny as a newborn nickel. The viewscreens showed no damage; only a bright, shiny mirror-surface which had been plated on the normal dull-white of the Earth ships by the metal vapor in vacuum.

"Mr. Barnes. Put us on a braking course and maneuver as necessary to match velocities with the Earth Fleet. Set the course to maintain a distance of five hundred kilometers."

"Aye, sir. At heavy G, sir?"

"Yes, Mr. Barnes. But not over four."

"Aye, sir."

Barnes would be disappointed by that last, Stan knew; but it couldn't be helped. No one yet knew what the top thrust capability of the new atomic beam was; but it was obviously well in excess of the four meters per second that it had so far been allowed to demonstrate. But this was no time to put his men, conditioned to lighter Gs, under more stress than necessary.

"No ladar signals, sir." Paulsen's voice was strained as he handled the console above his couch.

On the screen, the circle of ships was drifting past them, and then seemed to rotate as Barnes brought the *Phoenix* around in a match-course maneuver.

"They'll be moving away from us for about an hour, sir. And their ring is spreading. Shall I try for getting back to the stationary center?"

"Yes, Mr. Barnes. That should give us a good view of all of them. Are there any without spin?"

"No, sir."

"Good. Then they can't sneak a man outside for repairs without our seeing them."

Stan flipped his microphone onto another channel. "K-class pilots. Get your ships warmed up. You will be dropped as soon as we match orbits with Earth Fleet, and you will each guard a section of that fleet. Take no action unless an attempt is made to remove the mirror plating on those ships. If such an attempt is made, sting 'em till they blow."

"They don't seem to be operating very well, Star, those Earthies." Even Tobey's heavy-muscled throat seemed to be having trouble with the now constant four-G maneuvering thrust.

"Few ships operate well with all viewscreens, navigation equipment, and aiming devices out of service," Stan answered in what he had intended to be a dry tone, but what came out as a croak.

"That was the damnedest suckering move anybody ever pulled on them, Star." Tobey again.

Stan relaxed against the G-thrust. *We all need to talk out the tensions,* he decided, *no matter how great the effort to talk.* "I never was really sure they were stupid enough to be suckered in on it," he answered Tobey. "How much of that metal do you suppose plated out on them?"

"Probably not more than one percent." Stan could almost feel the implied shrug of Tobey's huge shoulders. "But ... where you have a cloud of metal vapor in a vacuum and a solid object for it to plate on, you can be darned sure that every atom that contacted them plated out. They haven't a viewscreen or a navigational instrument in operation—or any instrument on the surface of any ship, that is in useful condition now." There was a satisfied note in the croaking voice. "I wouldn't be surprised if it even sealed their air locks."

"How about common old radio, boss?" Paulsen asked. "Does it bother that, too?"

"It'll have plated out over the antenna insulators, too, and grounded them to the ships." Stan frowned in concentration. "They do have a system which uses the whole ship as a half-wave dipole. They might still be able to get through on that. Let's see. The ships are three hundred five meters long. Since they're operating on a half-wave dipole, that would put their radiation at six hundred ten meters. Or, say, right between four-ninety and four-ninety five kilohertz." He paused, then reverted to bridge formalities. "Mr. Paulsen. See if you can pick up Earth Fleet on the four-ninety to four-ninety-five kilohertz band."

Paulsen began twiddling the dials and snapping over switches, and after a few moments was rewarded with a thin, scratchy voice. ". . . peat. S.O.S. Flagship *Aurora*. We have been hit by a mirror bomb. Our circuits are"—the voice scratched and grew fainter, then came in more strongly—"screens blank. We cannot maneuver. . . ."

"Very well, Mr. Paulsen. Break in on them."

"*Phoenix* to Earth Fleet. *Phoenix* to Earth Fleet." Paulsen's voice had reassumed the crisp duty-tone of the bridge.

There was silence elsewhere as Paulsen's voice intoned the call, a little louder than necessary, Stan realized, for the benefit of the intercom. *Listen good, you guys aft,* he thought. *Listen real good, all of you.*

Abruptly the speaker on Paulsen's console came to life. It was a weak life, and the voice was scratchy.

"Commodore Rimes to *Phoenix*. We read you."

Stan pulled a microphone to him, nodded to Paulsen to switch the call over. Then he said: "Commodore Rimes. This is Star Dustin, Belt Commander. You are now blinded, and therefore I must warn you: you and your ships are safe only as long as you make no attempt whatsoever to send men onto the surface of any ship. Any ship on which figures appear will be blasted out of space. Otherwise, so long as you remain quiescent, you will not be harmed."

"Commodore Dustin. I hear you. We will give you our answer shortly." The voice was stronger now.

Stan grinned to himself. "Commodore Rimes," he said, "while you are considering your answer, you might consider the fact that I could sterilize everything in your fleet with my drive, if I wanted to. I do not plan to, but it is within my power. I could hit you with a megaroentgen-second blast from my drive tubes that would kill everything on board and sterilize your entire fleet. I repeat, I do not plan to do so."

There was a pause before the answer came back: "Commander Dustin. I have no choice but to take you at your word when you say that you will *not* sterilize this fleet."

"There would be no point to senseless slaughter, sir."

"Then I accept your terms. We will send no man to the surface until further notice. However, Earth cannot be too long patient with piratical actions. I hope, Commander Dustin, that you will come to the *Aurora* immediately to discuss the situation."

"Commander Rimes," Stan said grimly, "Earth Fleet was on its way to take over the Belt when we intercepted. The Belt has no quarrel with Earth, it is earth that is quarreling with the Belt. We will discuss the matter at our convenience, and will ferry you over here at that time. In the meantime, you will be safe *only* so long as you keep your men in board."

After he had switched off, Stan leaned back in his chair and rubbed his hand wearily over his eyes. Then he turned to Tobey. "Your K-pilots are not to harm any ship unless and until a man comes to the surface to repair damage. We don't want anybody taking out their desires for personal retribution."

Tobey nodded, his eyes on Stan.

"And, Tobey. Belt City will have to take care of Weed and whatever Earthie garrison he has stashed there. Can you alert them?"

"We'll take care of the clean-up job, Star," said Tobey quietly. "With Earth Fleet out of the way, there won't be too much of a problem in that. They'll be knocked out as soon as the boys on Belt City find out they're there. But, Star ... I don't guarantee there won't be what you call personal retribution in that operation."

The general, Commander Rimes, Stan and Tobey sat around the small desk in Stan's office. Paulsen, Sandra and Dr. Lang sat silent against the walls.

The general had lost none of his military bearing, and Stan found himself irrelevantly pleased with the fact. *There's a dignity about professional military men,* he told himself hopefully, *and perhaps some common sense. I'd hate to be dealing with Weed or Mallard,* he thought.

Then he turned to Commander Rimes and silent-

ly retracted the idea. Rimes was quite a different
breed of cat, even though probably a professional.
His bearing was arrogant rather than military; and
he was carrying it to the point of insolence. Frustra-
tion, Stan decided; and guilt. Both show.

"You understand what has happened, gentlemen?" he asked, opening the conference.

The general answered. "No, not really. We know
that you have knocked out a small army and then
Earth Fleet. I am not trained as a physicist, Mr.
Dustin; but I expect that the military will do well in
the future to put physicists into prominent posts. It
has been—well, technological thinking, I suppose,
by which the Belters have caught us by surprise
each time."

Stan smiled and shook his head. "You don't need
physicists, general. You need individualists.
Mallard and Weed were trying to give you robots;
and that was the worst sabotage anyone could
have perpetrated upon you. It takes a man who has
had to fight and win against his own hostile environment to be able to fight and win against the far
less serious opposition of an army or a space fleet."

Commander Rimes spoke up brusquely. "Whatever we may need, Commander Dustin, you may be
sure we will put our attention on it. Our question is,
simply; what do you hope to accomplish now? With
us?"

Stan looked him over carefully. "I hope to accomplish bloodless cease-fire and surrender terms
in which Earth admits the Belt's sovereignty and
withdraws all future claim to control of the solar
system."

The commander snorted. "You have, sir, in a
rather simple technological maneuver, blinded

Earth Fleet and now hold it helpless. You fooled me, Dustin. You won't fool us twice, of course. You have also, I gather, captured and now hold a small force of Earth soldiers, captured no doubt by some other unexpected system. But Earth herself is neither stupid nor helpless; nor do I think you can dictate surrender terms to her."

Stan raised one eyebrow, looking at the commander quizzically. "Earth is not helpless? Well, no. Earth is just scared," he said quietly.

As the commander started an angry rejoinder, Stan continued, "Earth has been afraid of space since the first Sputnik back in the mid-twentieth century. The powers that be on Earth have been so terrified of space that long after the means to actually reach the planets were fully known and carefully worked out, for at least a decade after power and drive systems were developed that made the solar system man's, they were kept top secret and the boondoggle of space rocketry on both sides of the Iron Curtain continued. Earth's establishment used every weapon at its command, from the top-secret label to murder and sabotage, to keep man *out of space* . . . because Earth is afraid of spacemen. And rightly so.

"But, gentlemen, *we* are spacemen. And Earth may fear us all she likes; she can no longer control us. The Belt will accept Mother Earth as an equal, but Belters will be no man's servants. Neither, as free men, do we wish to force Earth to her knees, though we are quite capable of doing so."

"Force Earth to her knees? Why, you pipsqueak commander of a one-ship armada, Earth does and must control the solar system. She—"

From the corner of his eye Stan saw Paulsen stiffen, saw Tobey half-rise from his seat.

Quicker than either of the other two, he leaned forward and his voice overrode the commander's his eyes fiercely boring into the—yes, frightened eyes, he realized—before him.

"You don't control any animal but a tame one, mister," he said, and his voice held the grimness of space. "And take this as a dictum: the men of the Belt are not tame—not to you, not to anybody. You don't tame space with tame men, mister.

"The Belt," he added slowly, "the Belt will not now, nor ever again, accept as much as a single gesture of domination from the tame men of Earth. And we have the means to back up our refusal."

Commander Rimes opened his mouth to answer angrily, but the general silenced him with a gesture, and it was the general who spoke quietly to Stan. "You have the means?"

Stan turned with relief to the professional calm of the other. He nodded slowly. "We have the means." Then he added bleakly, "It is a brutal means. We will not use it unless we are forced to do so. But neither will we let the weaklings of Earth use our ethical sense to enslave us. If Earth forces the question, we will not hesitate to be brutal."

Stan paused a minute, noting that the commander was holding himself in check only by obvious effort, then turned back to the general. "You've seen the *Phoenix* dive through atmosphere? On Jupiter, where the escape velocity is much higher than that of Earth?"

The general nodded, and Stan went on. "If this ship were taken to about five thousand feet and orbited Earth, only once, at say the forty-five-degree parallel, do you know what would happen?"

The general answered slowly, "There would be a rather major disaster from shock wave, I assume; and the forty-five-degree parallel would, of course, take you across the major population and governmental areas . . ."

"Yes," said Stan. "Shock wave. But not just major shock-wave damage, general, at the speeds at which this ship travels. Say a shock wave sufficiently deadly to kill anyone within five hundred miles on either side of the ground path zero. We wouldn't be breaking any nuclear-test-ban treaties. There would be no nucleonics involved whatsoever, other than the nucleonics of our drive. But the effect would be much the same.

"Where that shock wave touches ground, over a wide band that I have not yet estimated, well . . . how much of Earth do you think would withstand a blast of upward of a million degrees temperature? At that temperature, the very rocks would melt. And the ground-zero path beneath that shock wave would be as sterilized as any desert you now have.

"I doubt very much that Earth is prepared to pay for attempted domination of the solar system by such a disaster." 231

The general's face had gone white.

11

When man achieves control of his information input, analysis, filing, retrieval, and review systems he will release a tremendous proportion of the potential that exists in the vast files of knowledge he has acquired over the millennia.
  ——Findings in Centric Analysis
  #111864/77

The glowing veils of neon light with which Jupiter hides its face from the rest of the solar system danced and shimmered before them as Stan and Sandra stood outside on the nose surface of the huge wad-cutter bullet that was the *Phoenix*, staring up at the still distant but approaching planet.

"I knew it would be worth coming outside to see, but, oh Star, I didn't realize how truly beautiful it could be!"

Sandra's voice, even over the speaker in his suit, throbbed with a joy that brought a catch to Stan's throat. Then she added, "It seems a shame to dive into that. Are you sure we won't spoil the beauty?"

"Not much." He looked down at her trim figure in the P-suit tights that outlined every curve and detail. "We'll just look like a big streak of lightning —and be gone about as quick."

Her voice was hesitant then. "But, Stan. Why should we bother? Why have we come back? We've won. You're in control at A.T. The Belt is free. Earth won't try to enslave us again."

"What do you mean, 'won,' *Liebchen?*" Stan slipped his arm around the slender figure, holding her lithe suppleness close, though the bubble helmets kept their heads apart, and the heavy cloth of the pressure suits made a wall between them.

"Why . . ." She looked up at him, her face showing through the bubble, doubtful. "We *have* won, haven't we?"

He laughed, looking down into the bubble of her helmet, separating the blazing reflections from Jupiter on its surface from the stubbornness of her face beneath the clear plastic.

"In words made famous long ago, we've just begun to fight, you know," he said happily, a deep pleasure suffusing him as his old imp crept out from under the tensions and concentrations of the past months to make itself heard again. Then; "Sandra, Sandra —can't you see that we haven't won? Not yet? There will be tensions between Earth and the Belt for as long as there are only the two terminals—two groups of men with different ideas. The only answer is for us to go to the stars, so that there are lots of groups with lots of ideas; and so that those ideas and groups are so spread out that it's impractical, ever again, to get man bottled up into one little sys-

tem where his only way to let off steam is to clobber his nearest neighbor."

"The stars, Stan? I thought that was just . . . just the stuff of dreams. Just talk. Can the *Phoenix*. . .?"

"No. Not the *Phoenix*. Not to go to the stars. But —see that spark of light over there? That's one of Jupiter's moons. That's Io. And Io falls just within the mass limits necessary to make a planetary starship.

"It will take a few years to stock that ship, to get a colony going, to set up the necessary radiation belts and atmospheres, to build the small 'sun' that will be the focus of the magnetic vortex that will power and light our ship. It will take a few years to build her right. But we can do it.

"The equations are all there. They've been there since the mid-twentieth century. And it's time somebody put those equations to work.

"Sandra," he said softly over the speaker into her helmet, gazing up into the glory that is Jupiter, "Sandra, we can't stay planetbound, or Beltbound, or systembound. We're going out to where we'll be a quasar on Earth's telescopes. We're going out to join the other quasars that Earth has spotted in her telescopes.

"We're going to the stars."

A NOTE TO READERS

Those who enjoyed PHASE TWO will enjoy these other science fiction and fantasy titles from Ace. If any of them are unavailable at your bookstore you can order them direct from Book Mailing Service, Box 690, Rockville Centre, N.Y. 11571. Enclose a check or money order for the titles you order, adding 50¢ each for postage and handling. (If you order more than three titles, please include postage and handling for the first three only; we will absorb additional postage and handling costs.)

SIVA! by Walt and Leigh Richmond ($1.75)
Before THE CHARIOTS . . . Before CLOSE ENCOUNTERS . . . There was SIVA! A science fiction novel of the far past and the fast approaching present!

GALLAGHER'S GLACIER by Walt and Leigh Richmond ($1.95)
Blacklisted by the giant corporations of the corrupt space establishment, engineer N.N. Gallagher fights a lonely battle

to take control of space away from them and give it back to the individuals who first tamed it.

LEGACY by James H. Schmitz ($1.95)

Holati Tate made the epochal discovery of the Old Galactic plasmoids—and then disappeared. Trigger Agree was his closest assistant, and she means to find out why. And why did the long-vanished masters of the Old Galaxy exile the plasmoids to the most distant and isolated world they knew . . . By the author of THE WITCHES OF KARRES and THE DEMON BREED.

THE UNIVERSE AGAINST HER by James H. Schmit ($1.95)

The first novel of Telzy Amberdon, brilliant, charming, beautiful and the most powerful latent telepath the Psychology Service has ever discovered. Telzey could have a great future—if she weren't such an independent sort. As it is, her talent could prove disastrous to the Service—and they aren't good enemies to have.

THE DEMON BREED by James H. Schmitz ($1.95)

One young woman plays a deadly game with alien invaders. Andre Norton "could not put it down." *Analog* called it "another classic to match THE WITCHES OF KARRES." Schmitz is also the author of LEGACY and THE UNIVERSE AGAINST HER.

EXILES OF THE STARS by Andre Norton ($1.95)

In this thrilling sequel to MOON OF THREE RINGS, Free Trader Krip Vorlund and the Moon Singer, Maelen, continue their adventures on a planet where nameless evil battles with an ancient power.

THE GLORY THAT WAS by Sprague L. de Camp ($1.95)

A fascinating account of two men of the future in the Athens of Perikles, told by a master of historical fantasy.

DESTINIES #4 edited by Jim Baen ($2.25)

A blockbuster—the world's only paper-back science fiction magazine! "We never had so good an opportunity to recognize the talents of an editor . . . with DESTINIES, [Jim Baen] is editing the most attractive of the magazines."
—Orson Scott Card, in *Science Fiction Review*

THE ADOLESCENCE OF P-1 by Thomas J. Ryan ($2.25)

First mass market edition. *The New York Times* called it "part science fiction, part crime . . . a bang-up job . . . a scary novel very much of our own time." The best treatment of self-aware computer since

Robert A. Heinlein! Network radio campaign!

HOME FROM THE SHORE by Gordon R. Dickson ($2.25)

First mass market edition. The brilliant author-illustrator team of PRO does it again with an even more gorgeously illustrated story of land and sea ... and their inevitable clash. "One of the author's best alien cultures ... solid, well-paced ... enhanced by Odbert's pen-and-inks." *Questar*.

THE SPACE SWIMMERS by Gordon R. Dickson ($1.95)

The end of HOME FROM THE SHORE found Johnny Joya and his son striking out for a new life in the sea—and in THE SPACE SWIMMERS, they learn just what that will mean to all people, both Sea and Land. *With illustrations by Steve Fabian*.

SILVERLOCK by John Myers Myers ($2.25)

"Incomparable fun ... battles, feasts, drinking bouts, lovemaking, unabashed joy. . ." *Poul Anderson*. "I went through it like a tourist in Paradise." *Larry Niven*. "A Masterpiece!" *Jerry Pournelle*. A gigantic novel of fantastical frolic, with new, rave introductions by all of the above.

THE DOOR THROUGH SPACE by Marion Zimmer Bradley ($1.95)
The author of the world-famous DARK-OVER novels spins a thrilling tale of adventure under an alien sun.

TOO MANY MAGICIANS by Randall Garrett ($2.25)
Lord Darcy returns—and the Laws of Magic prevail—in this full-length sequel to MURDER AND MAGIC. "I cannot count the number of times I have read [it]—each time with the same pleasure." ANDRE NORTON.